TRANSFORMATIONS IN
THE RENAISSANCE
ENGLISH LYRIC

# TRANSFORMATIONS IN THE RENAISSANCE ENGLISH LYRIC

JEROME MAZZARO

CORNELL UNIVERSITY PRESS

ITHACA AND LONDON

*First published 1970*

International Standard Book Number 0-8014-0587-4
Library of Congress Catalog Card Number 74-124726

PRINTED IN THE UNITED STATES OF AMERICA
BY VAIL-BALLOU PRESS, INC.

*For Fred Plotkin*
*and Martin Pops*

# Preface

🍂 *Transformations in the Renaissance English Lyric* is a book about changes. It is not traditional genre or rhetorical criticism, nor is it properly literary history. It deals with the way forms of song become modes of vision and thought, and it tries to show how the shifts undergone by the English lyric in the sixteenth century from a musical to a rhetorical form are based on deeper changes in modes of seeing and thinking. As such, its concerns are with the history of ideas and are often tangential to the literary and musical works that one might normally expect such a book to investigate. Among the topics discussed are changes from medieval to Renaissance *res-verba* sensibilities, from Italianate to English modes of love behavior, from anonymity to self-consciousness, from symbolic to symptomatic views of music, from sixteenth- to twentieth-century concepts of the poet. The book touches, too, on the changing views toward the sixteenth century which critics have posited and, in outlining these views, gives a sense of primary relevance to even secondary material. Underscoring all of its discussions are the beliefs that the permanent products of the past—art, science, literature —must be seen in relation to what are likely to become the permanent products of our day and that the critic might do well to accommodate his views to the visions implicit in the lasting works about him.

In the Preface to the second edition of *Love and Death in the American Novel* (1966), Leslie A. Fiedler expresses the hope that "even the most casual reader will be able this time around to recognize the sense in which *Love and Death* can be read not as a conventional scholarly book— or an eccentric one—but a kind of gothic novel (complete with touches of black humor) whose subject is the American experience as recorded in our classic fiction." In so doing, he gives expression to a sense I first felt while constructing *The Poetic Themes of Robert Lowell* (1965). The nature of the material demanded a design which owed more to the chiasmic structure of Theodore Dreiser's *Sister Carrie* than to any established forms of exposition. Thus, as Lowell moved away from his early Roman Catholicism, the doctrinal (G. W. Hurstwood) and the experiential (Carrie) reversed their importance. Nor is fiction the only vision I found to which exposition might profitably attach itself. In constructing *Transformations*, I had the same sense that simple exposition would not do, but this time the forays of its separate chapters seemed to suggest, at least for me, the interpenetrating planes of cubist painting. The book's major concerns—the various transformations that the English lyric experienced during the sixteenth century—coalesced into an awareness of a complex transformation in consciousness involving a strange brand of flattened, ahistorical history and a liveliness of several voices contributing to the argument. These voices contributed a wider sense of materials and experience than I might normally have managed and seemed to compete for a reader's attention. So as to preserve this range and liveliness of several voices, I have used no superscripts or footnotes, but have provided references for the quotations at the back of the book. I have also modernized the spelling of the Renaissance prose I have used and I have tried in all cases to integrate the quoted material with the text.

That a book about transformations should itself participate in and contribute to a myth of transformation is not unusual. Yet, in offering it, I feel not like an Ovid but more like the modern counterpart of the pigmy Renaissance man standing on the shoulders of ancient giants, trying to reach a little higher than they. The book is so much indebted to ideas which have been dealt with by other people that it is to the high level of Renaissance scholarship as well as to any structure I might devise that I owe what higher reaches I may have gained. I began the book as an argument with John Williams' Preface to *English Renaissance Poetry* (1963), but in its course I came closer to Williams on many issues. I am also greatly indebted, oftentimes more than I give credit, to the wisdom of John Stevens' *Music & Poetry in the Early Tudor Court* (1961), though, it seems, we differ on crucial matters. In shaping the argument, I was aided by my colleagues, students, and friends, to whom I should like to give acknowledgment. They include Victor Doyno, Angus Fletcher, Jan Gordon, James Livingston, Laurence Michel, and Edward Snow. I should also like to thank James McKinnon for his suggestions on the music theory. I was aided in the book's completion as well by grants from the Research Foundation of the State University of New York that enabled me to take time off during the summer and write.

JEROME MAZZARO

*Buffalo, New York*
*July 1970*

# Contents

# Contents

# TRANSFORMATIONS IN
# THE RENAISSANCE
# ENGLISH LYRIC

# CHAPTER ONE

# *Res-Verba* Relations

Although occupied with a rather consistent view of love which was primarily its own, the English lyric in the sixteenth century was the product of manifold converging foreign and native traditions. Attempts to explain it or its structural transformations in terms of a single pattern, influence, or school consequently are likely to distort the character of the influences and minimize the variety of possibilities which at any time offer themselves to the writer. As critics are quick to explain, the sixteenth-century English lyric changed from structures which once permitted a "perfect" union of words and music to what in musical form became, in the Caroline court, formal aria and narrative recitative and to what, in literary form, became poetry written so as to exclude the possibility of its being set to music. Yet the method of these explanations leads generally into the neat categories which permit readers to get through an age quickly without reading it, by merely confirming the existence of certain trends. These categories have by their generalizing natures missed identifying the overall inner consistency of the changes. Such simplifications are themselves, as Neal Ward Gilbert suggests in *Renaissance Concepts of Method,* particularly "renaissance" in design: "The notion that method can provide a short cut to learning an art did not seem crucial to medieval students or educational reformers. Only when the milieu had become more time-conscious did method become the slogan of those who wished to speed up the processes of learning. . . . In the words of Girolamo Barro . . . method was the 'brief way under whose guidance we are led as quickly as possible to knowledge.' The insistence on speed is typical of the humanists; the arts must be learned 'as quickly as possible.' "

While such simplifications are the province of reconstructive literary history, itself a "renaissance" notion, and can rightly be discovered in many historical approaches to the century, to attempt an understanding of the transformations and their consistencies requires an approach similar to the dialectic which E. H. Gombrich reserves for *Art and Illusion,* that at any point in time the artist must create his work out of what the forms of his art have taught him to see and what matter his age has taught him to register: "Artists know that they learn by looking intensely at nature, but obviously looking alone has never sufficed to teach an artist his trade." Such an approach promises richer and more accurate results. It promises as well a clearer detailing of the assumptions that came in during the Renaissance and that are now being called into account, including the very idea of a Renaissance. While the knowledge gained thereby will be especially useful to specialists in the Renaissance, it may also serve to provide others with a better understanding of the present by revealing the nature of many of the assumptions which readers accept without questioning.

In *Literary Criticism in the Renaissance,* Joel E. Spingarn indicates that although its critics conceived broadly of three genres—"the lyric or melic, the dramatic or scenic, and the epic or narrative"—the Renaissance had no systematic lyric theory. "Those who discussed it at all," he notes, "gave most of their attention to its formal structure, its style, and especially the conceit it contained." Except in Germany where Horace was emulated, the model of all lyric poetry was Petrarch and, Spingarn goes on to indicate, "it was in accordance with the lyrical poet's agreement or disagreement with the Petrarchan method that he was regarded as a success or failure." He concludes that, as one consequence, the lyric genre remained more romantic and medieval than the dramatic and epic genres: "The tendency of Petrarchism was also in the direction of romanticism [i.e., medievalism]. Its 'conceits' and its subjectivity led to an unclassical extravagance of thought and expression; and the Petrarchistic influence made lyric poetry, and accordingly the criticism of lyric poetry, more romantic than any other form of literature or literary criticism during the period of classicism. It was for this reason that there was little lyricism in the classical period, not only in France, but wherever the classic temper predominated." With minor adjustments to these notions of a normative classicism and a subjective romanticism, variations of Spingarn's views are common in literary histories; yet such views do not take into consideration the vast amounts of knowledge of both the Middle Ages and the Renaissance which scholars have since amassed. This new knowledge obliges one to make a new inquiry into the nature of the literature, its function and place, and the function and place of the lyric and the lyric poet in the Middle Ages, as well as perhaps to redefine the nature of the lyric form before the Petrarchan influence in the sixteenth century.

First, if the Middle Ages conceived of creative literature divorced from philosophy and theology, writers did so only to consider its properties as a discipline or to condemn it by methods which were primarily nonliterary. Except for verbal mechanics, analyses of literature were moral and ethical and often insisted on discarding the literal, mimetic level of meaning for hidden, symbolic, and secret meanings. St. Augustine's distinction in *De musica* (A.D. 387, 391) between "art" and "imitation" proved indicative: "But if all imitation is art, and all art reason, all imitation is reason. But an irrational animal does not reason; therefore, it does not possess art. But it is capable of imitation; therefore, art is not imitation." Reason, not imitation, took precedence, and in literature words were thought of primarily as relating to realities outside the work rather than relating to other words within it. The sequence of these realities and not the flow of words determined a work's value. However attractive the tracery of their boughs, the literal trees of a forest disappeared for both writer and reader before allegorical types, and the

4

myopic, practical view which permitted the reader to react at the level of word and not at the remoter level of symbol was relegated to entertainment and oratory, not to poetry. Iconographies, based upon the "truths" of these allegorical relationships of word and thing, became established for most speculative disciplines and were used consistently by artists.

As Robert M. Grant suggests in *A Short History of the Interpretation of the Bible,* the history of the very notion of an allegorical method of perception conveys a rather one-sided, antimaterialist bias. The method was applied to classical literature by the Sophists and more thoroughly by the later Stoics. About the time of Christ, interpreters of the Torah adopted it, and St. Paul suggests it as a method of Christian perception in Galatians (4:22–26), where he speaks of the sons of Abraham as meaning "allegorically" the two covenants. He repeats the need for such a vision in 2 Corinthians (3:6), where he asserts that the "spirit" and not the "letter" will provide the understanding of the Old Testament. The method, with all its religious implications, was extended to Jewish history in the first century by the Hellenist Philo of Alexandria, and, in the first half of the sixth century, Fulgentius expanded it to include imaginative works as well. In his highly influential *Virgiliana continentia,* he pictures the *Aeneid* as a metaphor of life and the travels of Aeneas as the progress of the human soul from nature, through wisdom, to final happiness. "From this period," Spingarn observes, "the allegorical method became the recognized mode of interpreting literature, whether sacred or profane. Petrarch, in his letter, *De quibusdam fictionibus Virgilij*, treats the *Aeneid* after the manner of Fulgentius; and even at the very end of the Renaissance Tasso interpreted his own romantic epics in the same way." But behind Fulgentius and even Augustine is the work of Origen, who outlined the pattern of allegory when he interpreted scripture in the light of what was believed to be a tripart division of man by St. Paul into body, soul, and spirit (1 Thessalonians 5:23). Origen in *De principiis* surmised that there was appropriately in literature dealing with reality the same threefold division into a "bodily" or literal sense, a "soul" or moral sense, and a "spiritual" or allegorical-mystical sense. These divisions meshed early with Aristotle's tripart division of man's soul into vegetable, animal, and rational, and resulted in an interpretative flexibility combining theological and medical assumptions.

Thus medieval writers and critics were aware of at least two levels of word interaction in serious writing—a practical, "false," or rational relationship of words based upon "eloquence," and a deeper, symbolic relationship of words and things based upon "truth." Their awareness, rooted in *De doctrina Christiana* (A.D. 397, 426), absorbed Augustine's attempts both to moderate the Ciceronian tradition of a rhetoric based upon "eloquence" with the Platonic tradition of an eloquence and rhetoric based on truth and to integrate the work of the early Fathers of the Church by fusing the allegorical approach of Origen and the School of Alexandria with the historical approach of the more literalist School of Antioch. While preserving the basic Ciceronian questions (*an sit, quid sit, quale sit*) and the Ciceronian subjects of inquiry as concerned with realities and signs (*res et signa*), Augustine had insisted that the eloquence of words (*verba*) being themselves things, should not oppose the immeasurably greater eloquence of realities (*res*). To assure this proper *res-verba* relationship, he reduced the traditional Ciceronian five-part rhetoric of *inventio, dispositio, memoria, elocutio,* and *actio* into two parts: the *modus inveniendi,* roughly equivalent to the classical *inventio;* and the *modus proferendi,* mostly concerned with *elocutio,* but touching on *memoria* and *actio.* He also distinguished between eternal and temporal realities as requiring correspondingly different kinds of words, those which would be man-made and conventional, or language "in a widest sense," and those which would be internal and silent, by which in an extension of Plato's *Phaedo* (67), the inner teacher Christ would teach the truth. The allegorical demands of Paul were thus met by a rhetoric, which, like Origen's, culminated outside the literal work, but which did so principally to embrace a transcendent silence where the mind, aided by the Holy Spirit, might be in immediate contact with truth. Coevally, a basis was laid for the Church, protected by the Holy Spirit from false interpretation, to claim authoritative interpretation of such literature.

In the Augustinian compromise, where the purpose of serious literature becomes on a transcendent level the teaching of a uniform truth, a variety of writing styles on an immediate level became possible. Since the final value of each work would lie outside the author's style and the relationship of word to word, the writer's paramount consideration became the fidelity of his words or signs to a reality which he sought to capture and interpret. Recognizing this situation, Augustine reached two independent conclusions: that, although a speech or a piece of writing may be said to have a prevailing style, given a uniform truth, a mixture of styles is good for the sake of variety itself; and, second, that, because reality does not rely upon the agent of a single language, the greater or more truthful writings survive translation, not without some loss, but with their essential *res-verba* relationships intact. Since the eloquence of words may be used for both good and evil, Augustine, in deference to Cicero, would allow Christians to learn to be eloquent (*DDC*, IV,12,28). Basing his concession upon the idea that God, in order to be understood by all, speaks in "plain" style, Augustine designated the "humble" style of Cicero as best in teaching great things. He reserved the "moderate" style for praise and blame in regard to great things, and the "grand" style for persuading the reluctant in regard to great things. The attention which the writer paid to his style, therefore, inversely related to the truth of his content. His efforts increased as he went from a portrayal of truth itself in the plain style to the persuasion of others to truth in the grand. In establishing these roles for style, Augustine also cast into authoritative form the often verbalistic conceptions of allegory and history (typology, symbolism, and metaphor) which established for the Middle Ages the notion, elaborated by Fulgentius with regard to Vergil and evinced in the medieval commonplace tradition: all writings of lasting value are allegorical; they all are ciphers in some heavenly encyclopedia.

These concepts of allegory to which Augustine gave definition became further complicated in succeeding centuries. Going back to Origen, Gregory the Great ascribed three meanings to the Bible—the literal, the typical or allegorical, and the moral. Moreover, he extended "language" to include statuary. He defended church statuary against the charges of idolatry by asserting that statutes provided the "signs" whereby those who could not read might perceive reality. When, in the ninth century, biblical interpreters began to react to Rabanus Maurus' theory of the importance of the number four, a fourth meaning—the anagogical or mystical—was revived and inserted. "At a later date," Grant notes, "Franciscan number-mysticism encouraged the use of the fourfold interpretation. Many Franciscans considered all four senses of scripture to be of equal importance. Such Dominicans as Albertus Magnus and Thomas Aquinas, however, insisted that the literal meaning should be the basis of the other three." For his *Divine Comedy*, which he hoped would attain to truth, Dante boasted to Can Grande della Scala of attention to all four levels of understanding ("Epistola X," *c.* 1318). In creative terms, this claim implies a conditioning of art so that it rejects mere mimetic structures for words chosen to afford rational leaps from one level of understanding to another. This requires a language sophisticated enough so that words have both concrete and abstract potentials. As it evolved in the Middle Ages, such a language—

whether Latin or the vernacular—would complete structures whose inmost kernel was a *moralitas* and whose literal fable or poetic imaginings became the outside means to attract audiences to the hidden good. Writer and reader alike would conceive and riddle along religious and rational lines, making sure that language functioned on four levels, similar to the way in which modern psychological writers and readers now conceive and riddle literature along Freudian and Jungian schemes, making sure that language works on both a natural and subconscious level. Earlier in *De vulgari eloquentia* (*c.* 1304), Dante had named this sophistication "illustrious"—"something which shines forth illuminating and illuminated"—and claimed it for the Tuscan dialect.

These broad functions and distinctions of "moral" serious literature set up the boundaries for defining the lyric and the lyric poet. The definitions were consistent with the tale of Simonides told by Cicero and Quintilian. When composing his legendary song for the victors of the Olympic games, Simonides, the father of lyric poetry and of mnemonics, spent half of the song in praise of the Gemini. The microcosmic-macrocosmic correspondence implicit in these worldly (Castor) and divine (Pollux) twins became a commonplace for the bidirectional nature of the lyric genre. The Middle Ages preserved the correspondence when, in the case of lyric poetry, words were not differentiated from music, and evidence of its preservation exists in the treatises on music. Spingarn, who searches through Renaissance literary theory for clues to the nature of the lyric and not its music theory, is doomed from the beginning to find little about the special function of the genre. Had he consulted Augustine's *De musica*, on the other hand, he would have noted that the first six books of the unfinished treatise concern what today is considered poetry. The first five books discuss rhythm and meter, and the last deals with the cosmological and theological implications of numbers. Although not ecstatic in stress, the treatise does clarify "the hierarchy of numbers as constitutive of the soul, the universe, and the angels," and the direction of its implications is toward the *res-verba* distinctions of *De doctrina Christiana*. The proposed, unwritten six books would have dealt with harmony. In the sixteenth century, the complex methods of musical notation and the varied instruments that had begun appearing in the fourteenth century came under attack. Simplification was demanded. Scores written purely for instruments began to separate music and words, and writing about each became distinct. At this time, when lyric theory did, in fact, divorce itself from music, it moved into rhetoric with which it shared a use of tropes and colores, but not a common purpose.

Of the treatises which dealt with words and music during the Middle Ages, the most important and influential was *De institutione musica* by Boethius (A.D. 525). Purportedly about Greek music, it formed the heart of writing and teaching until well into the sixteenth century, when its theories on Greek music were superseded by the work of the Florentine *camerata*. Consistent with the last book of *De musica*, the treatise emphasized music as a *speculum*, a mirror of the universal order. The student of music contemplated a "hieroglyphical and shadowed lesson of the whole world." Boethius distinguished among three kinds of music: *in instrumentis constitua,* the music played by instruments or sung by voices, comparable to the "bodily" or literal sense of language; *musica humana,* the music of man's personality or of the body politic, comparable to the "soul" or moral sense of language; and *musica mundana,* the music caused by the motion of the spheres, comparable to the "spiritual" or allegorical-mystical sense of literature. Like the reality of words, the reality of musical notes did not exist properly in themselves, but the notes borrowed their meaning from a relationship to truth. Thus, played or sung music was the reflection on earth of God's arithmetic in heaven, a symbol of his order. By setting up sympathetic vibrations in the souls of men with the correct relationship between notes, music became not a passive but an active response to God. Even the most trivial music, such as John Skelton's witty "Devout Trental for Old John Clarke," was capable of transcendence, for, consistent with the poet's claims, *"Dulce melos / Penetra[t] coelos."*

As John Hollander notes in *The Untuning of the Sky,* this harmony, and accordingly its images of the harp and the lute—representative of lyric poetry—gave to the sixteenth century and Renaissance emblem books important symbols for the political state and for political harmony. The harmony conveyed by the emblems worked very much like the tuning of instruments: the poet derived from the *musica mundana* or *anima mundi* the right proportions that would, in the case of religious poetry, set the people vibrating sympathetically with the music of the spheres, or, on a social plane, vibrating sympathetically with the tone proper to the body politic. He did not so much persuade his hearers as enchant them away from any discord by evoking proper relationships. Charms against theft and work songs can even be seen as attempts to preserve or establish harmony on a primitive level. The lyric thus served the same basic function attributed by critics to tragedy—the ridding of antisocial feelings—but achieved its harmony by enchantment, not through the purgation of pity and fear (*katharsis*). For this reason, Plato admits the violent and peaceful functions of the lyric into his Republic. For this reason, too, perhaps, periods of great lyric poetry seldom have coincided with periods of great tragedy. In the Elizabethan Age, lyricism preceded the great tragedies.

Such a suprapersonal view of music encouraged treatises which refrained from suggesting that music become the expression of something as worldly as individual human emotion, and consistent with this fostering, writings of the fifteenth and early sixteenth centuries ignore music as an expressive agent. A polyphonic Mass or a motet was not written to make one feel good, but if it were written to God-given proportions, it could not fail to do so. For music was the art of right proportion, Augustine's *bene modulandi*, and if the composer's proportions were metaphysically right, then it followed that they were aesthetically right and that the moral results of their rightness would be good. Such music would put the little world of man in tune again with the Infinite. This accounts for the absorption of medieval music theorists in mathematical detail, and, unlike their counterparts in literature, for their apparent indifference to ethical results.

Moreover, at this time, neither the poet nor the musician proposed that the music accompanying the words should have a capacity or a duty to express the feelings aroused by the words. Both words and music took their designations from their religious and social roles and often independently followed complementary but separate conventions. Insofar as they did relate, their combined function was to transform the useless into the useful, the disharmonious into the harmonious, and the meaningless into the meaningful. Their combination was preferred to unsung music, and, because a musician could sing while playing the harp, the harp was preferred to the flute. God's natural music took precedence over all else. The Old English poem "The Phoenix" provides an excellent illustration of the order. In it, music is arranged in an ascending hierarchy of instruments (trumpet, horn, harp), songs (secular, then religious), and natural sounds (a dying swan, then "sounds created by God to give man happiness in this miserable world").

But being an incantation, music was susceptible to the evil influences of black magic, and opposed to the figures of proper music were the destructive Sirens and Satyrs. Set against the general praise for music were condemnations of the unaccompanied sound of wind instruments and reminders that both Plato and Aristotle had condemned the sensuous Lydian scale. As Gretchen Finney points out in *Musical Backgrounds for English Literature: 1580–1650,* early Church Fathers like Clement of Alexandria were quick to warn one to leave the pipe and flute to those inclined to idolatry: "We must be on our guard against whatever pleasure titillates eye and ear." St. John Chrysostom repeats this fear of the enticing musical sound and even qualifies his recommendations of sung music with warnings of the dangers of instrumental music. Not instruments but the Word of God has power over the soul, states Justin, and Jerome echoes him.

At the start of the sixteenth century, sung music could be grouped generally into political and topical songs, love songs, and songs on moral and religious subjects (including most of the carols). The groupings approximate Aristotle's view of man's life as vegetable, animal, and rational rather than St. Paul's tripart view of man. As cited by Dante in *De vulgari eloquentia*, "Insofar as man is vegetable he seeks for what is useful, wherein he is of like nature with plants; insofar as he is animal he seeks for what is pleasurable, wherein he is of like nature with the brutes; insofar as he is rational he seeks for what is right—and in this he stands alone, or is a partaker of the nature of angels." In such a system, what man seeks is "prowess in arms," "the fire of love," and "the direction of the will" respectively, and the pursuits are echoed in Sir Walter Raleigh's "The Soul" and in John Donne's "To the Countesse of Bedford. Honour is so sublime." Similarly, Edmund Spenser throughout his *Faerie Queene* (1590, 1596) considers poetry a speculum and offers as its purpose the same threefold aim. His *Amoretti* (1595) repeats the threefold division of man in its opening three quatrains.

Consistent with these functions of music and the definition of the lyric poem as a kind of incantation, the function of the lyric poet became that of a magician. He took his type from the established characters of David, Amphion, Orpheus, and Arion, much as Napoleon later would mythically confound himself with Alexander and Charlemagne, and as Christ earlier had fulfilled what had been written in the Old Testament. Like David's songs, the proper singing or song was able to soothe the evil spirits of a Saul; or like Amphion's, charm strewn and scattered stones into the walls of Thebes; or like Orpheus', animate lifeless and motionless objects; or like Arion's, compel a wild dolphin to bear him on its back. Since the poet's function was merely to provide this means through which the song might do its work, there was at the start of the sixteenth century little need for him to establish a sustained lyrical persona. As George T. Wright indicates in *The Poet in the Poem,* whatever else besides the instrument of song the poet may have been became irrelevant: "Thus a love sonnet does not present man in love, but man singing of love; an elegy is not a presentation of man feeling about death, but of man singing about death. The poet appears not as a man undergoing experiences but as man singing about his experiences."

In his Preface to *English Renaissance Poetry,* John Williams echoes this notion of the unmasked poet when he speaks of the native poet's almost always having spoken "from his own intelligence, as if he knew it existed." "He feels no compulsion to mask himself, to assume a persona, to work from cunning, or to live in exile. Speaking from his own intelligence, he speaks to another intelligence, as

lingly, insists that no man can be a poet unles
cian and that the better logician he is, the bette
l be.

nt any possible misconception, Varchi quickl
ogic and poetry differ in both their matter and
ments. The subject of logic is truth, arrived
s of the demonstrative syllogism; the subject
fiction or invention, arrived at by means of
ple (induction) or that form of syllogism
e enthymeme (deduction). The enthymeme,
d example of Aristotelian rhetoric accordingly
try. Moreover, involved with a common end
uman life perfect and happy, logic and poetry
heir modes of producing their effects. Logic
nd by teaching; rhetoric, by persuasion; his-
ation; poetry, by imitation or representation.
the poet thus became to imitate, invent, and
ngs which would render men virtuous and
se it did so not by precept but by example,
ed its end more perfectly than any other art
ill, because lyric poetry differed from both
and epic genres in that it did not generally
ced from the actual world—a false or fabu-
th its own sense of order, justice, and proba-
touched on it only slightly. Not being an
ife, of actions, or of men, lyric poetry re-
tgrowth and extension of life and society—
verbal vesture of an instant of emotion"—
perficially to rhetoric and poetry.

to these theories of music and of rhetoric,

if he knew that, too, existed; he is a reasonable man, ad-dressing with his own voice other reasonable men." Never, or rarely ever, did the poet appear as a full man "partici-pating in all the variety of life as other men do, with private interests and private business of his own," for to do so would have been to contaminate the purity of his own instrumentality. The poet's only business was song. Whatever he celebrated, he celebrated in his role as singer; for brooks and blossoms unsung were different from brooks and blossoms sung. The singing of them, Wright notes, was an assertion of their value, a transportation of them into a dimension peculiar to song where they became part of a harmonious whole.

If there was then this general consistency in theory as the English lyric poem moved into its split with music, there was also a consistent and equally complex tradition of rhetoric to which the lyric joined early in the century. Its emblems conveyed that this rhetoric converted the closed fist of logic into an exposed, open palm. It linked the learned with the lay world, the expert with the layman, the obscure with the commonplace. Hence the lyric's movement toward it represented another instance of what Paul Oskar Kristeller and Gilbert cite as the general ten-dency of humanists to encroach upon the speculative disciplines and make them persuasive. In *Renaissance Thought*, Kristeller cites specifically the humanists' at-tempts to invade the fields of logic and reduce them to rhetoric, and, in his book, Gilbert comments that "the number of school subjects 'brought into order' or 'reduced to art' during the late Renaissance is almost unbelievable."

In England, where since the time of Bede rhetoric had tended away from Augustine toward a "stylistic" rhetoric, an assumption prevailed that good style was a deliberate, systematic repudiation of the speech of everyday life and resulted only from word order that stood opposed to common speech. As Wilbur Samuel Howell notes in *Logic and Rhetoric in England, 1500–1700,* the emphasis of this rhetoric was on *elocutio.* The rhetoric evinced two characteristics: it openly admitted to a doctrine that style was the most important aspect of training in communication; and it openly allowed that invention (*inventio*), arrangement (*dispositio*), memory (*memoria*), and delivery (*actio*), or combinations of two or more of them, conceived of according to Cicero rather than to Augustine, were also legitimate parts of the full rhetorical discipline. This rhetoric returned the treatment of important matters to the grand style and saved the moderate and humble styles for lesser duties.

Moreover, as early as the twelfth century, John of Salisbury had merged rhetoric and poetry so that, when the idea of elocution—"the art of writing ornately the things already invented and arranged"—received attention in the literary theory of Geoffrey of Vinsauf, there were established precedents for it to build upon. In *English Literary Criticism: The Medieval Phase,* J. W. H. Atkins records that, consistent with the pseudo-Ciceronian *Epistle ad Herennium,* Geoffrey's *Poetria Nova* (c. 1210) lists ten tropes known as "difficult ornaments" (*ornatus difficilis*) to be used with the grand style for lofty themes. The more mechanical "easy ornaments" (*ornatus facilis*), consisting

of thirty-five figures of s
teen figures of thought,
ble styles which treated
fifteenth and sixteenth
increasingly to mesh wi
already established by tl
"propriety and splendo
adorned, in varying leng
French poet Pierre de
glitter like precious sto
lord."

Treatises written ear
that the framing of l
distinctions among the
spoken word as a "ra
strative (i.e., dealing
with the probable), ly
suasive and the false
and poetry. There the
toro deemed the func
essential beauty of tl
ideal, and to perform
accompaniment of b
minds of men in the
As Benedetto Varchi
poetry (1553), they s
neither strictly an ar
faculty. Only in the
rules and principles
fore him, Varchi clai

and, acco
he is a log
poet he w

To pre
notes that
their inst
at by me
of poetry
either ex
known as
"special,"
invaded p
of making
differed i
attained i
tory, by n
The aim
represent
happy. Be
poetry att
or science
the drama
create—d
lous worl
bility, cri
imitation
mained a
"the simp
bound onl

In addi

there was an equally complex and long tradition of writing to influence the vision of the would-be lyricist. He could preserve the degenerate "serious" mode of writing—the heavy, plodding post-Chaucerian poem with its many references to Chaucer, but with little of his artistry, urbanity, or vision. The form had become in the hands of these successors sprawling doggerel and its convention of dream allegory a pedantic device for prosiness and prolixity. The favorite vehicle of the poets was an "aureate" or "golden" style wherein they might disguise the thinness of their thought beneath a quantity of Latin-based, sonorous polysyllables. As Rossell Hope Robbins remarks in the Introduction to *Secular Lyrics of the XIVth and XVth Centuries,* their practice "spread downwards and, in the semi-official verse used at public ceremonies, became even more tiresome."

Side by side with this serious mode of writing and equally accessible was a popular tradition of humble style, which critics of the secular lyric term "native." Supposedly the style grew out of the short English poem of the fourteenth and fifteenth centuries and depended upon a "native" medieval tradition of grammar and rhetoric that worked with music and not against it. Robbins indicates that "by the fifteenth century the tricks and devices originally borrowed from France had become so native, that even a large body of verse showing signs of French influence would prove little; and there is no such corpus. Adornment confines itself to alliteration and refrain; and any unusual 'colores' or stylistic devices . . . can best be traced to the Latin rhetoricians." Yet such suppositions seem to ignore the effects of the tradition's origins on its continuing form as well as to presuppose a questionable concept of words and music as related directly to each other instead of related indirectly through a mutual focus upon a single object.

By contrast, the tradition before the year 1300 clearly points to an inability of the English Franciscan friars to absorb completely into Christian religious concepts either the troubadour and trouvère traditions from France or the lingering folk-tradition. As in other countries, these friars tried to instill Christianity by translating its concepts into the native language and by adapting popular, worldly, literary forms to suit their otherworldly purposes. M. J. C. Hodgart remarks in "Medieval Lyrics and the Ballads" that their lovely hymns to Mary still bear evidence of the sophisticated troubadour and trouvère songs in their elaborate rhyming stanzas, language of courtesy, analyses of the lover's emotion, emphases on refinement and humility, exaltations of the lady, and elaborate doctrines of courtly love. Equally, John Spiers notes in "A Survey of Medieval Verse," songs like "The Irish Dancer," "The Hawthorn Tree," "All Night by the Rose," and "Maiden of the Moor" preserve elements of their origins in the rites, ceremonies, and sacred dances of an old nature religion, and their possible evolutions in May Day celebrations. Even in several of the most beautiful Marian hymns, she retains something of the significance of the tree goddess, the flower goddess, or the spring goddess. In such carols as "There is a floure sprung of a tree," "Of a rose, a lovely rose," and "There is no rose of swich vertu," despite echoes of troubadour courtly love, the Virgin is more primitive than either the Christian symbol of the Rose or the tree out of which the Rose who is Christ springs.

Thus the polite tradition which began in Provence about the year 1100 with William IX, Count of Poitiers, cannot be discounted altogether. Although by 1500 the tradition had left in England very few examples of courtly lyrics and in these the courtly elements had been modified, it persisted in the stanza forms, conventional phrases, and subjects for poetry. Whatever modifications the clerics made and however prominent in them the English trait of alliteration appears, there remain as proof of a continuing influence openings which invoke the spring, analyses of unrequited love, and desires of lovers to be birds. In *The English Renaissance: Fact or Fiction?* E. M. W. Tillyard accepts the whole as a "blend of folk and courtly elements" and cites the merger as one of its main charms. "However much of the folk-*rhythm* may have penetrated into the mass of the English lyric," he insists, "the old folk-*themes* of the love lyric underwent a fundamental change. In the folk-tradition it is the woman who makes the advances; in the new lyric tradition it is the man, according to the new courtly convention imported from the Troubadours." Tillyard envisions this polite tradition as having been established "so early and so thoroughly that, when later the fashion for Petrarch arose . . . it implied no innovation but merely that an earlier convention was intensified and stylized." Although one should be cautious of Tillyard's contention that Petrarchism "implied no innovation," he, Hodgart, and Spiers come closer than Robbins to understanding the effects on an artist's vision which the persistence of forms suggests, however much they may have been "naturalized" before the sixteenth century.

To this combined folk and polite tradition were added in the thirteenth century literary imitations of various kinds of folk songs. The imitations became popular first in northern France and then in England, where among the older forms emerging with newly simplified scores were the "aubade," or song of the lovers' separation at dawn; the "pastourelle," originally a seductive encounter between a knight and shepherdess; the "reverdie," such as "Sumer is icumen in," which celebrates the return of spring; the complaint of the ill-bred wife; and the lament of the nun. In common fashion, the poet, in the role of moral observer, rode out in the morning to meet a shepherdess, or overheard a pair of courtly lovers, or recorded a woman complaining about her husband. Rather than the elaborate rhyme schemes of the troubadours, however, these imitations used a simple dance-song with refrain, imitated quickly in turn by the religious poets. Furthermore, in the fifteenth century, the discant style received new stimulus from the religious music of John Dunstable, who by creating a plastic, convoluted line refashioned fifteenth-century music. This refashioning, though not immediately or directly picked up by his English successors, comprised both adopting from thirteenth-century French composers a shift from the tenor to the treble as the governing line and a more careful control of dissonance. The first eliminated what in "The Early Renaissance" Brian

Trowell calls "the stern voice of authority which governed the medieval motet," and the second proved essential for the development of the new choral polyphony. Moreover, cross-rhythms under Dunstable's influence gave way to a flowing, unitary meter of "perfect time."

Nevertheless, for the would-be lyricist, the most insistent new development of the English lyric before the Tudor period would have been the quick evolution of the fifteenth-century carol. By simplifying the elaborate stanza and rhyme schemes of the troubadours, this form revived "carolling or ring dancing" and threatened in its popularity to submerge most other forms. Coming before the ballad and the religious and secular lyrics of the sixteenth century, it provided the transition between these forms and their predecessors.  According to some critics, caroling may have been part of an old nature ritual which antedates the Christian Church and which may have been preserved by such outlaw elements of society as witches. On social, historical, and philosophical grounds, Margit Sahlin counterargues for deriving the words "carol" and "carole" not from the Greek "choros" and related words but from the expression "kyrie-eleison." Her *Etude sur la carole médiévale* asserts that the phrase, familiar to everyone before the Reformation from its use in the Mass and in the litanies, was a popular acclamation and widely used as a refrain in popular poetry. In *A Social History of English Music,* E. D. Mackerness suggests another origin. He proposes that the carol, like the troubadour songs, may have been imported from Provence, where since William the Conqueror there had been close, continuous contact:

"The best-known form of sung dance was the Carole which as danced in Provence had two main forms, the Farandole and the Branle [English "brawle"?] or Round Dance. English contact with Provence was close in the twelfth and thirteenth centuries; dance melodies were no doubt heard and repeated by English merchants and political emissaries returning from the Provençal region." Whatever its actual origin, the seemingly sudden appearance or reappearance of caroling in England in the fourteenth century prompted the author of "Sir Gawaine and the Green Knight" to take notice of it as significant and new.

According to Richard Leighton Greene in *Early English Carols,* the carol as it was taken over by the clerics was a song of joy accompanying a dance and differing from a hymn by promoting God's glory in creation rather than by ascribing glory to Him. The form was somehow allied to the Franciscan *lauda,* or song of praise, as well as to the folk song, and by its generous use of Latin it evinced a heritage from the accentual Latin hymns of the Middle Ages. In general, carols were the work of authors who could wield macaronic or bilingual verse. The sense of the line moved smoothly from English to Latin to English, carrying forward the same subject matter. Expectably perhaps, the most famous writer of carols, James Ryman, was a Franciscan friar of the Canterbury House. This strong connection of the carol with clerics led in the fifteenth century to the form's becoming a song not actually accompanied by dancing and to an association with Christmas. By the year 1500, "carol" meant "song." Yet, what would have distinguished the carol from other forms of

Middle English lyrics for the aspiring lyricist would have been its burden—the presence of an invariable line or group of lines which is sung before the first stanza and after all stanzas. Not part of the stanza, but wholly outside an individual stanza pattern and a member only of the carol as a whole, the burden differed from the refrain, which, in the art song, remained a member of the stanza.

Greene also sees three principal points of difference between the carol and the ballad which succeeded it in popularity and which some scholars believe may have been derived from it. These differences may be reduced to the manner of transmission, the narrative sense, and the metrical form. By definition, the ballad has become a narrative song which combines ellipses and repetition to tell a tale, and there makes an end. The stress of its transmission is on the tale, not on the emotions of the teller or his hearers, nor on the teller's relationship with his audience. The objectivity of the ballad remains one touchstone of its authenticity. Now, neither complete objectivity nor narrative content was essential or even usual in the carol. Moreover, the narrative sense of the carol was typically that of a known story entirely lacking in suspense. It was told for a religious, moralizing, satirizing, or immediate purpose, and hence differed widely from the ballad. The narrative sense of the carol differed from the ballad also by not being the product of a sustained process of oral transmission impinged upon here and there by faulty memories, improvisations, and multiple and widely circulated copybook versions. The third point of difference, that of metrical form, offers some unsolved questions but can still serve valuably as a practical means of distinction: unlike the ballad refrain, the carol burden could stand rhythmically divorced from the stanza pattern.

As Hodgart adds, and important for a lyricist, the special narrative technique of the ballad would carry a "folk-view of life, an ironic acceptance of tragedy, and a rich background of popular myth, of ghosts and fairies." Only occasionally would it penetrate the court. Robbins concludes that "in a number of ways the close of the fifteenth century prepares the way for the Tudor and Elizabethan lyrics with the rise of 'gentlemen' poets, the formation of literary fashions, such as the love epistle and the catalogue of charms, and the heightened interest in poems of a single stanza, which prepared the ground for the acceptance of the Italian sonnet form." Thus, besides having a varied tradition of sources from which to draw both its structures and subjects, the lyric before 1500 had set philosophical and social systems applicable to both music and words which minimized individual expression. The lyrics that remain show an overwhelming preference for the humble style of plainness (*tenuitas*), simplicity (*simplicitas*), and confidence (*securitas*). In *Music & Poetry in the Early Tudor Court,* John Stevens indicates that the beginning of Tudor lyrics marks no real break with previous forms, for the century still continues the medieval carol and the post-Chaucerian lyric.

Of the already cited catalogue of the lyric's three general forms, both the religious and love songs could be further subdivided. The religious lyric fell into the clerical carol, which was complex and ornate, and dwelt with dramatic intensity on the physical and spiritual anguish of the Passion; and the popular carol, which was rough and direct, and combined a warmth of human feeling with a matter-of-factness and a sense of wonder. The one was solemnly devotional; the other, didactic and gay. Likewise, the love songs which elaborated the time-honored chivalric themes of absence, desertion, departure, and service, offered two styles: the post-Chaucerian rhyme-royal stanzas (ababbcc) of courtly verse; and lighter, courtly love poems written in common measure, in four-line stanzas with three or four stresses to each line.

Still, for one sensitive equally to words and music, the change in thinking which established the reality of both words and notes and thereby made possible their conflict could have been most disturbing. For with the separation, the mutually exclusive ideas of musical and literary embellishments which set in during the sixteenth century, but which had been evolving long before, could gain ground. During the fourteenth century, Albert Seay writes in *Music in the Medieval World,* interest in the speculative nature of music was already declining. He attributes the decline "to an overpowering fascination with technical novelties and lessened dependence of such innovations upon philosophical justification." "Indeed," he goes on to say, "many works suggest an impatience with the older need to begin with a speculative foundation. Several treatises of the fourteenth century have as their opening phrase, 'Gaudent brevitate moderni' ('Modern men rejoice in brevity'), and then proceed without further ado to the practicalities that are the purpose of the exposition." In the sixteenth century, two trends in embellishment resulted. There was, on one hand, a constant and successful effort to make the texts in vocal music more easily understandable and to make music immediately and strikingly express the images and especially the feelings suggested by the texts. At the same time, the rise in instrumental music bore witness to the urge to create musical forms which could be complete and satisfying as purely musical entities without the support of words. Both trends, for example, led the Councils of Basel (1431–1437) and of Trent (1545–1563) to complain that the musical structure of contrapuntal Masses diminished the meaning of words, an irritation which the humanist Erasmus was to register in his translation of the New Testament (1519) particularly against English church music: "Modern church music is so constructed that the congregation cannot hear one distinct word. The choristers themselves do not understand what they are singing, yet according to priests and monks it constitutes the whole of religion. . . . In college or monastery it is still the same: music, nothing but music. There was no music in St. Paul's time. Words were then pronounced plainly. Words nowadays mean nothing. . . . If they want music, let them sing Psalms like rational beings, and not too many of those."

Coevally, the popularity of the sixteenth-century lyric would no doubt demand its having to affect a grander, more important style, if for no reason other than the growing ethical and moral emphases which English humanism and Puritanism placed upon literature. Unlike the Franciscans who had at the time of their transformation the support of a plain Augustinian rhetoric, the new rhetoricians would have to lend their energies to "difficult" tropes and colores. Moreover, as Dante's calling the Italian counterpart of the lyric—the *canzoni*—the highest form of the vernacular poetry suggests, the conditions for the revaluation of the lyric in England in the sixteenth century may have been part of a general European movement to preserve the primacy of words above music and to let the music take its lead from the poet's contemplation. Certainly that had been the case in Italy, where in *L'Ercolano* (1570), Varchi had insisted one employ only the most restrained and nonvulgar words for the lyric, citing Dante and Petrarch for the consecration of the genre.

But equally important to this growing sense of dissociation is what composer Aaron Copland in *Music and Imagination* describes as the opposing effects of music and poetry. Basing his distinction on a concept of time in which the present does exist as an entity different from the past and the future, he writes: "This never-ending flow of music forces us to use our imaginations; for music is in a continual state of becoming." He opposes this flow of music to the flow of words, which he feels is reflective and forces the reader to stop and think. In short, the effect of music upon a listener is anticipation—a listening for what is to come; and the effect of "verse glittering like precious stones" is arrest—a listening for what is to come only in relation to what has been. Poetry thus combines two processes—anticipation and recollection—into a unified experience. This added, "psychological" effect, which makes the judgment of opera difficult, precludes any ex-

31

tended, satisfactory, artful combination of the forms. As Stevens suggests, "Nothing in the history of the changing relationship of music and poetry up to about the year 1500 suggests that the composers or poets idealized the union of music and poetry." He sees their relationship at various stages as "natural," where words and music cannot be separated by memory; as "utilitarian," where music is employed as an aid to memorization; and as "abstract," where abstruse systems of notation make music independent of words.

Although not responding particularly to either Copland or Stevens, Wilfrid Mellers in "Words and Music in Elizabethan England" takes issue with the idea of a natural antipathy between words and music, insisting that the separation of the two arts is comparatively recent and that the link between them is "rooted deep in human nature." He agrees, however, that the dissociation was "part of the growth of the professionalism in both arts." "In Shakespeare's day there was an increasing tendency for the professional musician and the professional man of letters to become distinct." He sees this tendency as a working toward music written for instruments and away from music written for voice. "Inevitably a creative musical culture which puts the main stress on the human voice must imply an intimate connexion between words and music." He sees this connection evolving in France and in Italy into opera, but in England finds no such comparable consummation. "The closest approach to it was in the collaboration of Ben Jonson, Alfonso Ferrabosco the younger (c. 1575–1628), and Inigo Jones in the production of masques." Here, however, the elements of musical drama remained undeveloped. "The reason for this," Mellers conjectures (contradicting his own basic assumption of a "deep-rooted natural" link), "may have been that the court culture in England was more deeply impregnated with popular elements than it was in France and in Italy." In *Music and Society*, Mellers clarifies this stand by indicating that once the naïve "natural" link between words and music is broken, words and music can only become naturally joined again through the device of a sophisticated self-conscious stylization. In one sense, then, his position is similar to that taken by theologians regarding the innocence of Adam: once having fallen into sin, he requires a state of self-consciousness before he can regain God's likeness.

Printing practices in the sixteenth century also apparently contributed to the dissociation. High production costs prevented large printings of music and lyrics until well into the century. Ottaviano dei Petrucci's *Harmonice musices Odhecaton A,* the first book of part music to be printed from movable type, appeared in Venice in 1501, and the first collection of printed instrumental pieces—four books of lute pieces, chiefly dances—appeared six years later. In 1528, Pierre Attaignant began issuing printed musical texts in Paris, and, in England, printed musical texts date from 1530. John Day continued the interest with *Certain Notes* [1560?, 1565], but not until the publication of William Byrd's *Psalms, Sonnets, and Songs of Sadness and Piety* (1588) did printed music gain popularity. As M. C. Boyd conjectures in *Elizabethan Mu-*

*sic and Musical Criticism,* "The printing of Elizabethan anthems and service music could not have been profitable. Not only was the market too small, but there were no copyright restrictions to prevent choirboys from copying the music for almost nothing. There is no way of finding out the prices of Elizabethan printed music, but . . . few choirs could have owned any." This prohibitive cost of printing words and music together was reflected in Richard Tottel's *Songs and Sonnets* (1557), from which most of the Elizabethan poets learned their craft and, in turn, learned to communicate with readers. The collection did not contain any music for its song lyrics and unlike its successors, *A Handful of Pleasant Delights* (1566) and *A Gorgeous Gallery of Gallant Inventions* (1584), it did not list the popular ditties to which the lyrics might be sung. Tottel apparently believed the words could stand alone and in the case of some Wyatt lyrics revised them away from their unions with music. As a consequence, an entire generation of poets grew up viewing song lyrics without their music and shaping their own efforts to the page representations of these songs.

In *Elizabethan Lyrics,* Catherine Ing cites as philosophical justifications of Tottel's page representations the possible influence of Pico della Mirandola's *Liber de imaginatione* (1501), which Sir Thomas More had translated into English. The treatise makes the visual property, rather than Dante's aural property, the archetype of all sense experience. It reflects the new spatial awareness which had been part of Filippo Brunelleschi's painting and which had formed Leone Battista Alberti's *Della pictura* (1435).

There Alberti established the ability of the eye "to seek after the most fugitive aspects of things" and "to show the movements of the soul by means of the movements of the limbs" as well as laid down his views on perspective, which shaped subsequent art and geometry. Miss Ing offers as indication of Pico's effect two distinct precedents which *Songs and Sonnets* established. First, she finds, writers and printers carefully set out their work visually to enlist a reader's understanding of how the letters were to be translated into aural images in the mind. Conventions of punctuation, capitalization, italicization, and paragraph spacing became a means of indicating not only logical relationships but also the proper modulations of the voice. The reader could thus approximate the author's intention. Second, she notes, writers and printers encouraged the practice of mingling long and short lines in various verse forms, which continued throughout the period. The convention enabled the eye to signal to the mind some expectation of the proportions which were to be heard by the mind's ear. Further, its eye-appeal made the reading of a poem a pleasurable experience for two senses. Accordingly a printed poem became a small work of art or craft, designed to be pretty and attractive in every possible mode. "In this way, too," she concludes, "printing had a little effect on the structure of the poems as well as being affected by it. Acrostics are essentially a result of seeing, rather than of hearing."

Williams' summary of the results of this union of words and music as it evolves into the sixteenth century is apt. The subject of the Tudor poem "is usually broad and generic and of what we might call persistent human significance; the purpose to which the subject is put is instructive or informative or judicial." However, he does not explain that part of this manner of broad and generic language may be the result of the music, for as Rosemund Tuve points out in *Elizabethan and Metaphysical Imagery,* William Butler Yeats, who did not have the philosophical background of the Renaissance, is led "unexpectedly" by song "to generalized imagery, highly traditional in character and somewhat out of keeping with the poetic purposes generally assigned to him (of which accurate representation of states of mind is certainly one)." Similarly, Mellers suggests that "music is of its very nature a generalizing art" and leads to generalized rather than specific detail in poetry. "Many of the conventions in Elizabethan lyric poetry which seem to us frigid and unconvincing were hardly intended to be self-subsistent. In the ayre, even more than in the madrigal, the words serve merely to evoke an appropriate musical response; the literary convention is completed only in the musical convention, the music being an essential part of the expressive significance of the words." The dissociation of words and music, as it became more pronounced in the course of the century, could only evolve into a growing self-sufficiency on the part of both disciplines.

# CHAPTER TWO

# The Message and the Medium

🍁 Both Hugh M. Richmond's *The School of Love* and J. B. Broadbent's *Poetic Love* suggest that Freudian theory forms the current measure of love in the English Renaissance lyric. Evincing Freud's basic reductionist logic, the measure supposes that things are what they can be reduced to. In the matter of emotion, things are reduced to sex or to sex sublimation. To argue with the accuracy of such a reduction would be foolish, for much of the love poetry of the Renaissance is a hopeful preface to seduction, and in the selection of the sonnet form the poets were consciously obliged, according to Dante and Sir Philip Sidney, to deal with man's animal being. To persist narrowly in this area, however, or to insist upon rigidly applying the reduction either to the love conventions or to the literature without taking into account other social, aesthetic, and philosophical implications is to do the poetry a great disservice. By ignoring the relevance of such observations as La Rochefoucauld's that many people would never have been in love if they had not heard love talked about, everything becomes a monotonous ritual. It would be comparable to reducing the human body to its chemical components and treating man as chemical. Not that this reduction would, in fact, be false, but it simply ignores the subject's vaster, more interesting, and more various characteristics.

Since man's sexuality, as Irving Singer asserts in *The Nature of Love: Plato to Luther,* "does not exist apart from thinking, feeling, doing—and above all, the making of a system of values," the source of love can never be merely God, nor the libido; it must also include the ideas about love which have evolved throughout history. Gaining prevalence in one period, these ideas retract into the presuppositions of another, retaining always at least the residue of animal instinct. Preferably, therefore, a critic should perhaps suspend his current presuppositions about the "real" nature of love and, before he too quickly categorizes or perverts all views of love according to Freud, George Santayana, or even to Singer's own bestowal-appraisal system, openly give a hearing to the rather consistent view of love about which the changing structures of the sixteenth-century English lyric formed.

The love conventions of the English Renaissance lyric derive from conceptions of the poet and the courtly poem that date at least back to the troubadours. In these conceptions, the poet is essentially both a court historian and a court entertainer. If asked, he immortalized the day's events or provided the material for an after-dinner occasion where members of the court might sing, play instruments, or dance. His pieces were social behavior and art equally, and they were filled with the stock formulae that attach to both formal social behavior and impromptu composition. Since the qualities of a courtier—self-restraint, self-control, and self-mastery—were those that were taught by love, the poet could use his skills to elaborate a logic of courtly behavior which centered on love. His logic began with an observed and fundamental premise that falling in love made man pleasing to others. From this, the first deduction, Stevens notes, is that if one wanted to please he must allow himself to fall and to remain in love. The second is that, if one wanted to please and were not in love, he must act the lover. Vital to pleasing in either instance was "goodly speche," which gave the courtier an opportunity to display his polish with the opposite sex, both by reading tales of love and by employing his own rhetoric to praise and to persuade.

Yet, as E. Talbot Donaldson indicates in "The Myth of Courtly Love," one is not to assume that in England this behavior necessarily led to illicit intercourse. Strictures against such a final step were common, and the implicit notion of a higher kind of love outside of marriage was not offered. Rather what was extended was a view of man's ethical behavior in a social world based upon the example of love. In this respect, J. W. Lever in *The Elizabethan Love Sonnet* points out that despite occasional touches of gaiety, the great majority of the English lyrics that survive the Middle Ages generally "view love as pitiable and frail, at the mercy of wind and weather." "Even when no moralizing tone is heard," he goes on to note, "the true

English love lyric shows none of the southern tendency to idealize or apotheosize the girl who is wooed. Courtship is simple, sincere, a pledge of quiet partnership through life. And most frequently of all, the conclusion is drawn that roses, romance, and the desires of summer are light things to set against the onslaught of winter and death." Lisle John in *The Elizabethan Sonnet Sequence* indicates that "the representations of love found in English verse before the appearance of Tottel's *Miscellany* are largely those of the medieval period rather than of the straight Ovidian interpretation."

Even after the advent of Ovidian concepts in *Songs and Sonnets,* the contents of *A Handful of Pleasant Delights,* aimed mainly at the middle-class Englishman, illustrate how entrenched the ideas of constancy of married love and the impermanence of romance were in the sixteenth century. "A Proper Wooing Song" presents the expected ideas of true love and the pledges of quiet partnership through life. "A Sonnet of Two Faithful Lovers" offers true lovers who, like Pyramus and Thisbe, prefer death to life without each other. "A New Sonnet of Pyramis and Thisbie" deals specifically and sympathetically with the famous lovers who, rather than separate, do commit a kind of senseless, dual suicide. "The Complaint of a Woman Lover," in contrast, emphasizes constancy by demonstrating the fickleness of romance. It announces that "All men are false, there is no choice" and that new love can put "the old to flight." Similarly, "I Smile To See How You Devise" warns that "though thou makest a fainèd vow, / That love no more thy heart should nip, /

Yet think I know as well as thou, / The fickle helm doth guide the ship." Whether dalliance, then, was fact or fiction in these courtly circles has little impact upon the strategy of the love lyric since, in keeping with the virtuous and happy demands on poetry, only marriage assured the listener of constancy.

*A Handful of Pleasant Delights* also makes clear that other equally important ideas on social behavior were current. Although perhaps not indigenous to England, they had by the start of the sixteenth century become part of her thinking. First, repeated time and again and reflecting some of the views of the Medieval Church, was that reason can successfully oppose love. In *The Allegory of Love,* C. S. Lewis traces the history of these Church views, beginning with Gregory the Great, who at the end of the sixth century defined the act of love as innocent but the desire as morally evil. As corollary, he offered a righteous rebuke delivered in anger. Later, Peter Lombard located the evil similarly in the desire, but said that it was not a moral evil. It was merely a punishment of the Fall. Thus, the act, though not free from evil, might be free from moral evil or sin, but only if it were "excused by the good ends of marriage." In the work of Albertus Magnus, the desire as man knows it is an evil, a punishment for the Fall, but not a sin. Finally, in its Thomistic form, the theory acquitted the carnal desire and the carnal pleasure and found the evil in the suspension of intellectual activity. "This is almost the opposite of the view," Lewis states, "implicit in so much romantic love poetry, that it is precisely passion which purifies."

Consistent with these views, *A Handful of Pleasant Delights* repeatedly advises that, if Cupid's darts chance to light, one raise up reason (intellect) and that, if reason fails, one then either recognize he is in the midst of false love or choose the occasion to fall back on the "excuse" of the good ends of marriage. Under such a view, the villains to reason were two: women, who tempted man to the loss of reason; and fancy, which fed the loss. Thus, in "A Warning for Wooers," one is counseled against being "snared with lovely looks" by being advised to choose wit (reason) and leave will (desire). In "The Lover Compareth Some Subtle Suitors to the Hunter," ladies are warned against leading false men into such fancy as would make them fall in love, for by such actions they may be bringing about their own undoing. Ultimately, as moral law demands and as "Dame Beauty's Reply to the Love Late at Liberty" shows, each individual is morally responsible for his torments in love. He has only his wanton will and idle mind to blame for his discomfort, first for letting himself fall in love and then for letting his fancy hold sway. In true love, it is to be supposed, there are no cruel torments and no long separations of reason and emotion.

The book also conveys an implicit relationship between the soul in such states of unreason and the body affected by the impacts of love. Its descriptions of the existence of fantasies that a lover permits himself form part of a long-believed-in, medically recognized "lover's malady." John Livingston Lowes in "The Loveres Maladye of Hereos" (1914), John Charles Nelson in *Renaissance Theory of Love* (1958), and Robert Burton in *The Anatomy of*

*Melancholy* (1621) treat of such views of illness in the early and late Renaissance. Like the desire which prompts it, the malady seems to be a result of the Fall. It has clearly delineated symptoms, signs, and cures, culled from literatures, treatises, and testimonies, and these do not seem to have changed much in kind since the second century before Christ. Descriptions of the illness—the lover's chills and fever, his compulsive behavior rooted in a separation of reason and emotion, his rapid changes in color and mood consequent upon the nature of his fantasies, his languishes and losses of appetite—are commonplace in the poetry, as are many of the cures—hard work, song, a journey, purges, diversions, and potions. Like the religious concepts of love, these medical views cross into every day life and offer Tudor England ways of remedying love's torments when reason cannot be resummoned.

Lastly, the book establishes in the popular Tudor imagination elements of a courtly tradition, but one not so corrupt as that proposed by an uncritical reading of Andreas Capellanus. In keeping with the notion of the ethical bias of the example of love, this tradition would reward the dalliance of women with leprosy and death. Still, in courtly rather than folk convention, it offers man, not woman as the aggressor. It likewise offers in poems like "Greensleeves" elements of service. Doing nice things can persuade a girl to fall in love, although, as "Greensleeves" indicates, she may not always do so. Not in the collection and courtly in tone, Wyatt's poetry offers a similar service and failure. It shows the common belief, stated or implied, that good appearance and good actions enlist favorable results. In fact, this belief often leads Wyatt to complain when the results are not what he considers "fair."

Although, as John indicates, the love poetry in *Songs and Sonnets* tends to be less English than previous love poetry, no tendency to apotheosize the woman exists here. However married she may be or above the poet in station, she is hardly unattainable, never morbidly long-lamented, and never an agent for religious reformation as are Dante's Beatrice and Petrarch's Laura. John Donne's later elegies for Elizabeth Drury provide a possible exception, but contemporary attacks upon them by people like Ben Jonson merely affirm the un-English nature of such exaggerated laments. Like the stress upon the active in all areas of Tudor life, Tudor love poetry, as it formed a model for social behavior, tended in its conclusions to be more active than contemplative. When a woman serves the function of reformation as does Stella in Sidney's *Astrophel and Stella* (1591), she merely sends her lover away; she does not die. In Shakespeare's *Much Ado About Nothing* and *The Winter's Tale*, the "dead" women—Hero and Hermione—are "restored" to their repentant lovers after the changes have been effected to produce happy ends.

Baldassare Castiglione's *Il cortegiano* (1528), taken up by the century as a manual of courtly behavior and translated into English by Sir Thomas Hoby in 1561, made it clear that courtly romance, regardless of delight, simply set the stage for the more speculative concerns of art and philosophy. The poets of the Tudor court, however, found progressing beyond an intermediate stage of talking, dancing, games, and sport to a philosophy of love difficult. Stevens notes that this stage of social intercourse—"the game of love"—most intently appealed to the Tudors. This is not to dismiss the religious and moral poems of a poet like John Skelton, nor the metrical psalms of Wyatt and other Tudors, but to indicate that as the works are speculative they occupy a place of less interest than the love lyrics, as in the previous century the love lyrics were less important than the carols. This reformation through love is perhaps another manifestation of the humanists' appeal to a moral world through the "arts" of courtship. In the face of this appeal, Sir Thomas Elyot in *The Defense of Good Women* (1545) tries to make this humanistically based definition of social behavior an end in itself. He has Candidus speak of true lovers in terms conveying no more fervency than polite conversation: "Nay, truly; true lovers, of which company I confess myself to be one, are in no part of their condition. For only delighting in the honest behavior, wisdom and gentleness of ladies or other matrons, we therefore desire to be in their companies, and by mutual devising to use honest solace." Hollander also suggests some of the new aggrandizement of the moral realm, noting that dancing in the court grew in importance: "The dance as courtly entertainment becomes associated with music in general only during the sixteenth century in England; previously the actual dancing (aside from its music, which was not considered at all as anything but popular music of the lowest kind) would have been considered a branch of games rather than of music."

45

Also clear in this intermediate stage of courtly behavior is that, in the failure to absorb the justification of the continental beliefs in philosophy or to form a comparable native justification, the poet would have to rely upon his inherited native beliefs. Despite whatever upgrading by the court, the attraction between a man and a woman remains vaguely subjective, magnetic, and illustrative of what Singer calls "bestowal." The woman's attraction never becomes a matter of objective dimension as it is for Petrarch, for beauty never becomes so formulated as to be a matter of objective perception. It remains, rather, a sense of satisfaction. If a lady is kind, she will win a man's love and seem beautiful; if not, she will appear unattractive because of her harshness, and he will not risk involvement. Thus, at about the same time English scientists were offering the world the principles of magnetism, magnetism was being offered by her poets as a basis of love. This lack of progress beyond the game of love may explain why English poets never developed an image of beauty based upon native qualities to replace those proportions of beauty which the Italian poets outlined, and why, in retelling the Hamlet story (1886), Jules Laforgue sees Ophelia's love for Hamlet as akin to a Hobbesian view of property.

On the other hand, there is little reason to suppose that when poets engaged in these courtly games of love, their speculative failures led to a presentation of dalliance as anything other than what it was, nor to suppose that their presentations went unrewarded. Morality was never inhumanly enforced in the court circles of Henry VIII, and

seeing love as a physically defined activity that was governed exclusively by sexual attraction or reaction and that was directed toward physical consummation. The Greek elements of romantic love, which had been directed toward the male and away from the business of procreation, remained in England at least a minor theme. Anacreontic influences hit late in the century. Thus, for England, the Latin love conventions of the tradition represented the major Tudor importation. Here, the primary issues of love tended not toward delicate, marginal discriminations, and the logic was simple: the girl was to surrender physically; betrayal meant physical union with a rival; and suspended consummation was a challenge to arouse sexual appetite. If one were to be warned about women, one was told that they were fickle or, like Clytemnestra and Phaedra, deadly, not that they were sinful or agents of evil. In a writer like Ovid, who exerted a great influence, love was frequently depicted as a god of irresistible power—a tyrant who tortured his victims cruelly or punished them with great severity. This harshness was at times treated as the god's vengeance upon those who resisted his will. He was provided with arrows that could wound the hearts of lovers; he could also kindle fires in their breasts. Yet, unlike the Christian view which saw these actions as destructive of man's will and strength, Ovid's god, however capricious, could inspire men with great courage and significantly increase their power.

The Tudors never officially questioned Ovid's belief that lovemaking itself was a science or art that must be learned according to certain rules which he laid down in

*Ars Amatoria,* for, as Gilbert has indicated, the century was spent generally reducing actions to rules. But there is no evidence that the Tudors widely practiced these rules. The four principles which Ovid had set down indicated that, contrary to the native view, true love lay outside of marriage. For Ovid, love had to be illegitimate, furtive, and accompanied by fear. A calm, quiet, assured love was no substitute for the interest and fascination of risk. Furthermore, the lady should be capricious; her yielding must be preceded by changeableness, haughtiness, and unjust treatment, for possible loss added zest. Lastly, the man must be ready to endure hardships or to perform difficult feats in order to win his lady's love or to get into her presence. As influential as *Ars Amatoria* was Ovid's *Remedia Amoris.* Here, he turned doctor to administer to the disease he had written of as an art. In what were already traditional medical terms, he distinguishes this lovesickness from all other diseases by its being at the same time pleasant and painful, and exhibiting symptoms of paleness, trembling, fear, loss of appetite, sighing, sleeplessness, weeping, crying out, fainting, and mental absorption that often led to rash actions and the loss of senses, insanity, and even death. The disease, according to Ovid, could be cured only by the return of the affections of the lover.

During the early Middle Ages, the beliefs of this continental tradition were codified, and the remedies for lovesickness took on at least a variety consistent with Christian behavior. This codification, Lewis notes, marked a significant change in thought concerning the relationship between men and women. The change altered four areas of the relationship—humility, courtesy, adultery, and the religion of love. It least affected the medical treatments of love, including the *Remedia Amoris,* carrying these treatments basically unaltered into the new code. The importance of the codification was that it opened behavior in love to public discussion and objective analyses, something completely lacking in classical poetry, though present in Platonic and Neoplatonic philosophy. This public discussion, by making behavior in love subject to clearly outlined, approved methods, ultimately made possible in the Renaissance the substitution of love poetry (poetry of example) for religious poetry (poetry of correction).

The Moslem influences in the Sicilian court of the Emperor Frederick II soon diminished adultery as a theme of public discussion. Women did not have to be married 'to other men before poets could address them. These modifications reached the Italian mainland through Guittone d'Arezzo, Rinaldo d'Aquino, and Guido Guinicelli, and England through the more influential writings of Dante and Petrarch, but not before the love conventions had undergone further changes. In Guinicelli's mature poetry, the inner workings of his love for his lady replaced the outer course of his love, and with these inner workings, the marginal discriminations of love begin. As significantly, in Guido Cavalcanti's poetry love leads to death, but not before it has forced him to undergo suffering that is only rarely redeemed by slight recognitions from the lady and that, however much rationalized, never loses its sting. Unlike love in the native English tradition, in these writers it proves permanent. Additionally, for Dante as later for

Petrarch, love effects a religious transformation through symbolic investments, resolving by a chasteness the conflict between the teaching of the Church and the worship of an earthly lady. As Richmond indicates, "In the true troubadour tradition, both Beatrice and Laura are married to other men, and neither shows much passion for her lover; but the poets manage to compensate for the lack of intimacy and responsiveness by endowing the women with symbolic qualities." "Both women," he goes on to note as the game of love turns into philosophy, "represent for their admirers an expression of those moral ideas with which the poets are increasingly concerned at the expense of personal and sexual matters." The degree to which they become symbols has been argued by scholars, particularly regarding Laura. Nevertheless, there are "obvious analogies to Plato's theory of love, by which cruder sexual relationships form only a preliminary incentive to more spiritual and ultimately purely intellectual ones."

These analogies to Plato's theory of love are later heightened in the continental tradition by the *trattati d'amore* so as to become permanently allied. In "The Metaphysic of Love," A. J. Smith's summary of the public discussions indicates that sixteenth-century Italian writing was not "all of a Neoplatonic piece." "As well as the Platonic Florence of Ficino there was the Aristotelian Padua of Sperone Speroni, not a whit less in following; and besides both there was the great synthetic source on which all subsequent sixteenth-century theorists, of all complexions, drew heavily, the *Dialoghi d'Amore* of the Spanish born Italian Jew, Leone Ebreo (Jehudah Arbadnel)." In brief, the Italian schools differed in the degree of importance each assigned to the body (realism) in love. For the Ficinians, the ascent of love was away from the body, through as many as five stages. For the Aristotelians, two categories of love prevailed: "vulgar love," whose end was simply the enjoyment of the body; and "honest love," which was generated not in desire but by reason. Instability characterized the former, and a loss of semblance for the attainment of a strange third species (neither male nor female) marked the latter. It remained for Ebreo to add to this transformed union of souls "the ecstasy, or else alienation, produced by amorous meditation," and to make this ecstasy "a mystical sharing of some part of the Divine Beauty and Wisdom."

Since most of these treatises on love originated from discussions either of the *Canzonieri* or the work of the Petrarchans and Petrarchisti, the qualities of the tradition, amassed into the "Petrarchanism" which challenged sixteenth-century England from abroad, were far more extensive than the mere range of Petrarch. They may be summarized briefly as an idea of true love, but not in marriage; an idea of love as gratuitous, capricious, and overwhelming (Reason cannot be summoned to counteract it); an idea of love as an illness (a surfeit of fancy); an idea of the permanence of love even after death; an idea of women as saintly because they purify; an idea of love as an attraction to proportion, so much so that an ideal woman can be prescribed; and lastly an idea of love as nonsensual. The first three qualities are attributable ultimately to Ovid; the other four are later additions. The seven may be

seen as opposing the basically native notions already speci-
fied of an idea of true love, but only in marriage; an idea
of love as the wilful suspension of reason; an idea of love
as an illness (self-induced by fancy); an idea of the tran-
sience of love (no morbid languishes); an idea of women
as evil because they tend to cause the suspension of reason;
an idea of love as magnetism wherein a woman is beautiful
because she is in love and not beautiful because of physi-
cal proportions; and finally an idea of love which ulti-
mately involves sexual intercourse.

Thus, by the time England was ready for Petrarch, a
sufficient immunity to the social and philosophical presup-
positions of his poetry had been established so that, even
with the stress on artificiality which the court poets af-
fected, they were not able to succeed in a complete en-
grafting. Assuredly the themes were there: the cruel mis-
tress, golden-haired, with lilies and roses contending in her
cheeks; and her faithful lover, alternately hoping and
fearing, at once freezing and burning. Likewise, the
Petrarchan situations: the lady walking, sitting in the gar-
den, playing on a musical instrument, sighing, or falling
sick; the lover comparing himself to a sea-tossed ship,
invoking sleep, promising eternity or fame through his
writing. There are, too, the continual searches for com-
parisons worthy of the lady's beauty and grace; frequent
requisitions of the four seasons, the heavenly bodies, legen-
dary heroes and ladies, gods and goddesses, kings and
kingdoms; addresses to the Muses, the moon, sleep, high-
ways, joy, life, death, and air; usages of the law court and
signs of the zodiac. Nevertheless, as Williams points out,

54

in their use "subject and theme have drawn so far apart that only by an act of rhetoric can they be reunited." He goes on to complain that "the solidity, straightforwardness, and restraint of Native style . . . has given way to an airy elegance, which does not so much support the substance of the poem as it decorates it, to a style distinguished by the ingenuity of its figures, a rapid association of details, a wordplay meant to dazzle rather than inform, a diction that was faintly archaic and 'literary' even in its own time, by an elaborate syntax, and by the varied and subtle rhythms resulting from the play of that syntax against the poetic line." In *Sir Thomas Wyatt,* Sergio Baldi states the conditions more succinctly: "The truth is that the world of Petrarch's imagination remained closed to Wyatt."

This inability to respond fully to Petrarch's world led the early English Petrarchists to reproduce those Petrarchan sonnets and ideas that were most natively English. Their decision, moreover, seems justified; the Tudor audience could hardly be expected to be any more receptive than they themselves to the themes of the Italian poets who had progressed beyond an intermediate stage of Castiglione into philosophy or any more tolerant of the "wanton" Italianate behavior implicit in the themes than the English prose writers. In addition, despite the contention of Robbins, the early Tudor poets, as Lever has indicated, were not sufficiently skilled themselves in the techniques of short poems. This lack of skill is certainly true of Skelton, less true of Wyatt, and a personal disposition seems to have worked to defeat Surrey. The poets consequently selected sonnets that were uncomplicated in structure and that dealt with love as an illness or with the proportions of beauty. In the first instance, they charted the course of love's pains and pleasures. In the second, they catalogued. Thus, the common criticism lodged against them, that they often did not translate the best Italian sonnets, begins to assume a more appropriate context. In the absence of a real world out of which "verbal vestures of instants of emotion" might proceed without a persona, the poets created a false, compromise world—neither Petrarch's nor their own—where, as in the narrative and epic genre, the speaker might assume a role and over which a closed system of poetic justice would rule.

A poet like Skelton (1460–1529), whose earliest poems are written in an aureate, post-Chaucerian manner, manifests the failure of sufficient preparation for the short poem as well as many of the forces at work on a court poet at the beginning of the century. He uses both a short-line, accentual verse based in the late medieval Latin poem and a native, popular folk-tradition to enlarge upon man's moral and animal life. Religious, moral, and love poems proliferate, an understandable mixture perhaps for a cleric who spent most of his time in and out of the court circles of Henry VIII and who, if the scandalous tales of him are true, was not immune to the successes of the courtly manner. Many of these songs have a monodic chant line, based either upon a model of the Gregorian chant or a system of musical accompaniment similar to that proposed for Anglo-Saxon verse. All show the evolution of a remarkable range of musical forms and of musical knowledge.

The early love lyrics present Skelton's themes of sexual disappointment and emotional betrayal not in works of one stanza but in troubadour song structures debased by folk elements. Like Wyatt's later loves, these loves are either beyond his reach or turn into common whores. Two of his best lyrics, "Mannerly Margery" and "My Darling Dear," treat sex with a frankness that is common in the English tradition but which becomes rarer after the advent of Petrarchism. The first lyric recounts a dialogue between a man and a woman in which the woman is wooed and left. The second complements the account with a tale of a wife who kisses her amorous husband to sleep and then skips off to her lover. Looking forward to Wyatt's similar treatments, a third early lyric, "To Mistress Anne," offers the conditions for continuing service and love. All display a general view of love inherited from the Middle Ages.

The later lyrics of resignation add to Skelton's early frank view of love a limpid, expansive tenderness and vernal simplicity, but as yet no Petrarchism. Typical of the lyrics written in honor of the various ladies assembled in Sheriff-Hutton Castle, "To Mistress Margery Wentworth" betrays an almost pure folk-song structure in its abab rhyme scheme, three-stress line, and ballad refrain, in addition to a tradition of nature in its inclusion of various flowers. Yet, as W. H. Auden in "John Skelton" has remarked of both periods: "His best poems . . . are like triumphantly successful prize poems. The themes . . . have all the air of set subjects. They may be lucky choices, but one feels that others would have done almost equally as well, not, as with Milton, that his themes were the only ones to which his genius would respond at that particular moment in his life; that, had they not occurred to him, he would have written nothing. They never read as personal experience, brooded upon, and transfigured."

"To Mistress Anne" illustrates most precisely what the love lyricist offered a pre-sonnet Tudor court. The song is indicative of what Williams cites as the poet's "speaking from his own intelligence, as if he knew it existed" and "feeling no compulsion to mask himself, to assume a persona, to work from cunning, or to live in exile. Speaking from his own intelligence, he speaks to another intelligence, as if he knew that it, too, existed." Besides a number of measures in each stanza identical to the fourteen measures of a ballad stanza (4–3–4–3), the song shares with Wyatt's subsequent songs two qualities. First, it employs a variable number of syllables within what seems to be a fixed musical measure; second, it creates a tension within the stanza by varying the duration of words. Each stanza begins slowly with three lines that outline a condition and closes with a more rapid statement of the consequences. Assuming that those parts in italics receive a duration twice that of the parts in roman type, and those in capitals three times those in roman type, one can derive some sense of the effect which, set to music, the alterations in rhythm might achieve:

Mis·*tress* / ANNE, /
I *am* / your *man*, /
As *you* / may *well* / ES- / PY. /
If *you* / will *be* /

Con·*tent* / with *me*, /
I *am* / your *man*. /

But *if* / you *will* /
Keep *comp-* / 'ny *still* /
With ev·'ry / knave *that* / COMES / BY, /
Then *you* / will *be* /
For·*sake-* / 'nof *me*, /
That *am* / your *man*. /

But *if* / you *fain*, /
I *tell* / you *plain*, /
If I pre- / sent·*ly* / SHALL / DIE, /
I *will* / not *such* /
As *loves* / too *much*, /
That *am* / your *man*. /

For *if* / you *can* /
Love *ev-* / 'ry *man* /
That *can* / flat·*ter* / AND / LIE, /
Then *are* / YE /
No *match* / for *me*, /
That *am* / your *man*. /

For I will / not *take* /
No such kind / or *make* /
(May *all* / full *well* / IT / TRY!), /
But off will / ye *cast* /
At *an-* / y *blast*, /
That *am* / your *man*. /

Like the ballad, the song keeps to the "easy ornaments"
(*ornatus facilis*), which Geoffrey of Vinsauf had restricted
to the humble and moderate styles. It does not share in
the *contentio* of the later Tudor lyrics, where favorable

and unfavorable values are opposed, but relies heavily upon various kinds of repetition for its effects. Indeed, there is in it, as generally in Skelton's work, a singleness of tone that makes it seem to be what most medieval carols and chants are—an extension and variation of a musical phrase. The internal oppositions of emotion and oppositions of stanzas which come in later to approximate more nearly the vacillations one now expects of thought may be an added refinement of court sophistication and cynicism, or even a refinement of Wyatt. The kinds of repetition the poem relies upon are classed by Geoffrey under both figures of speech and figures of thought. Under the first heading, the poem uses mainly *repetitio* (repetition of a word at the beginning of successive clauses or sentences), *traductio* (repetition of a word elsewhere for emphasis), and *conduplicato* (repetition of a word to express emotion). Under the second heading, to support and illustrate a principle with similar, accumulated examples, it uses *expolitio* (enlarging upon a topic in different ways).

In the *Epistle ad Herennium*, the function assigned to these figures of speech is to make a work more tightly knit, so that they approximate what in modern critical terminology would be techniques of texture. The tightness of this texture is increased through the *expolitio* which, by allowing each stanza to be a thematic extension of the first, also makes the movement of each extension identical. This identical movement fits neatly the repetition demanded by the strophic structure of song, where the music accompanying the first stanza accompanies all other stanzas, creating an even more tightly knit piece.

Choosing not to go back to medieval terminology, Alan Swallow in "Skelton: The Structure of the Poem" redesignates aspects of this repetition as the "accumulative method." His source for such a redesignation may well have been Philip Henderson's comment in his Introduction to *The Complete Poems of John Skelton:* "Over and over again he repeats the same things, devoid of all logical form and construction—although these pieces may be said to have certain concentric movement of their own—round and round the same point he goes, always coming back to where he started from."

Some of these same qualities of repetition and of a debased troubadour lyric can be seen in "An Inconstant Mistress," which predates Skelton. The lyric comes closer in theme to Wyatt's songs, and, upon it, H. A. Mason in *Humanism and Poetry in the Early Tudor Court* bases a contention that Wyatt's lyrics mark no significant improvement over the lyrics of the previous century. He points out that for the most part "they are in a convention: but the convention is linguistically bad and bad in sentiment." While granting that they reject "aureate diction" and "the massive use of French words, particularly strings of rhymes in -aunce," he notes that the poems also reject "the particular and the new, or rather, do not attempt either." He finds, in addition, Wyatt's sentiments are all too monotonous: "If the lover is complaining, he is all complaints, if he spurns service, he is all scorn." An extension of Lever's objections, Mason's position opposes the more common view that, as Maurice Evans phrases it in *English Poetry in the Sixteenth Century*, Wyatt's successes and originality lie in his having "crossed the love lyric with the deeper psychological realism of Chaucer and transferred the interest from the outer situation to the inner drama of the mind."

But before even an examination of "An Inconstant Mistress" can be essayed, a more thorough understanding of the principles of lyricism based upon a practical understanding of words and music and of syllabic irregularities in addition to the previously discussed ideas of ornamentation in the humble style must be formulated. This formulation is not easy. It negates an idea of flexible rhythm in poetry which the ear has learned to detect and which defeats so knowing a critic as Tillyard. In discussing Wyatt's "With Serving Still" (Muir, #157), for example, he not only assumes that metrical stress changes in each stanza, but he bases much of his interpretation upon these changes:

> With serving still
>   This have I won,
> For my goodwill
>   To be undone.
>
> And for redress
>   Of all my pain,
> Disdainfulness
>   I have again;
>
> And for reward
>   Of all my smart,
> Lo, thus unheard
>   I must depart!

Wherefore all ye
That after shall
By fortune be,
As I am, thrall,

Example take
What I have won
Thus for her sake
To be undone!

"Nothing could be better," Tillyard writes, "than the dramatic emphasis of *'This* have I won' and *'Thus* for her sake,' or than the skill with which 'Disdainfulness' is made to occupy a whole line, suggesting a choking mouthful of very dry biscuit instead of the refreshing drink the lover had hoped for. Moreover the speaker is half acting. He puts on just a little more indignation than he really feels in order to make his advice to the audience to take example by him the more effective. In fact the humour and the elegant conversational tone are not only new, but look right forward to the witty sophistication of the court lyric of a century later."

In "The Lyrics of Wyatt: Poems or Songs?" Winifred Maynard proposes that the lyric fits the popular "Taunder naken" and may well have been sung to it, but even if it were not sung to that particular tune, the stress which Tillyard puts upon "This" in line 2 and "Thus" in line 19 is unlikely. To stress both words would throw any musical structure off. In addition, the musical accompaniment for "disdainfulness"—whether or not choking as he suggests—is repeated in "Thus for her sake" as well as "For my goodwill," and in the former would seem indeed inappropriate. If any irony exists—and the equation of good and evil with the same musical phrases suggests that one may—it lies in the speaker's realizing that evil comes of good, in his exploding the naïveté which believes that good begets good and that his serving is, in fact, "goodwill" (for whom?) and not a kind of scheming disguised as goodwill since obviously its lack of results betrays a foiled ulterior purpose. Tillyard is, however, correct that the equation of lines 2 and 3 of each stanza carries the burden of the irony. As for the poem's looking "forward to the witty sophistication of the court lyric of a century later," it should be pointed out, as R. G. Cox points out in "A Survey of Literature from Donne to Marvell," that the Caroline lyrics "are more independent of music; even when obviously songs, their evolution is not so closely controlled by the needs of the composer. Their use of language is close to cultivated speech, their imagery is more intellectual and less sensuous, their method is often dialectical, and they aim at classical neatness and point."

Likewise, Mark Van Doren in *Introduction to Poetry,* while justifying the syllabic irregularities of Wyatt's "They Flee From Me" (#37) so as to make it superior to the metrically regular but tampered version that appeared in *Songs and Sonnets,* chooses to account for the irregularities in every way but the most obvious one. Set to music, the irregularities can easily and quickly be absorbed by the score. His conclusion is correct: "Wyatt's meter was perfect as it stood. The time of each line was right, however many syllables had been suppressed. When a syllable was missing, another one, or several others, pronounced themselves slowly enough to make up the difference." But it also betrays the nonmusical basis of his argument. It is perhaps a better conjecture that Tottel was not familiar with the tune to which the lyric was sung and sought to revise the lyric accordingly, for, as Stevens indicates, copybooks seldom contained the "ayres" to which the lyrics they contained were to be sung, and Tottel, unlike his successors, never prefaced an ayre by the title of its "dittie."

Support for such an explanation has already been suggested by Miss Ing. Writing in particular of Wyatt's "What Shulde I Saye" (#143), she concludes:

It is true that other parts of the stanzas do not seem to carry out the perfect repetition of stressing which I have suggested as a distinguishing feature of air poetry. The second line is the obvious difficulty here. In the first stanza it has four syllables, in the second and third stanzas five syllables, and in the last stanza only three. It might be that "It is not my mind" was to be taken as " 'Tis not my mind," but this does not help to explain "And you promised me" or "But you said." I think the explanation is to be found in the very fact that the apparent difficulty occurs always in the same line.

"It suggests," she goes on to note, "that a musical phrase for this line might be one using either running short notes which could carry either one whole syllable or only a part of a syllable, or long notes which could be divided where more syllables were used. The structure of these stanzas, in fact, shows clearly that mingling of freedom and control that writing for airs could give. There is a place (here in the second line) allowed for license, a kind of Saturnalia, which is not permitted to disturb the order of the rest, and in fact, helps to emphasize that order." However, Miss Ing nowhere notes the ironic effects produced by singing "So will I trust" to the same melodic phrase as "With doubleness" and "Your double heart," nor the ironic effect of lengthening the notes of the three-syllable "But you said," emphasizing again the "doubleness" of the lady's actions. The irony suggests the poem's social-games character which genially corrects by example rather than by lecture.

The irony, which is consistent with Wyatt's life and "innate melancholy of temperament" as defined by Baldi, is not typical of "An Inconstant Mistress." Nevertheless, it does take a folk song meter of eight syllables divided into fours that is often used by Wyatt and evinces the same native, un-Petrarchan attitude toward the woman, who is neither apotheosized nor eternalized by his love. Still utilizing, like Skelton, the "easy ornaments" of repetition rather than *contentio,* the poem is monotonous in its sentiment:

> O Mestres, whye
> Owtecaste am I
> all vtterly
> from your pleasaunce?
> Sythe ye & I
> of thys, truly,
> famyliarly
> haue had pastaunce.
>
> And lovyngly
> ye wolde aply
> thy company
> to my comforte;

But now, truly,
vnlovyngly
ye do deny
　　Me to resorte.

And me to see
as strange ye be,
as thowe that ye
　　shuld nowe deny,
or else possesse
that nobylnes
to be dochess
　　of grete Savoy.

But sythe that ye
So strange wylbe
As toward me,
　　& wyll not medyll,
I truste, percase,
to fynde some grace
to haue free chayse,
　　& spede as welle!

Here the poet, as Baldi has indicated of Wyatt, "gives us no genuine meditation of the nature of love. When he is not interpreting it as the personification of a hostile Fate, or a torturing madness, he sets about making it, curiously enough, the basis of a theory of rights." This "theory of rights," which the author of "An Inconstant Mistress" and Wyatt share, affirms the ethical nature of the Tudor love lyric rather than the lack of originality which Mason wishes to assign to it or the personal idiosyncrasy of Wyatt which Baldi derives.

But this is not to disagree with Baldi's other conclusions regarding the "wellspring" of Wyatt's poetry. As he rightly states of Wyatt:

Something in him makes it impossible for him, as least as a creative artist, to be happy in his love; and because he is moved to poetry only by the negative side of love, that is, by love checked or unvalued or lost, he is able to give vivid expression not only to the torments he has suffered for his lady but also, with equal intensity, to his own pain at not being able to return another's love. . . . Moreover, since love always comes to him in the guise of suffering, Wyatt regards the state of not being in love as a freedom which he has wrested from Fate. He writes songs exulting in his liberation from love's tyranny; and these may seem at first to be substitutes for those poems of happy love we have so far failed to find. . . . These poems rather suggest exaggerated demonstrations of relief and triumph.

The sentiments are even more significant, given both the extent of the turmoil in the Tudor court and the fact that love represented for Wyatt social behavior. His wanting to be free of love's tyranny may have had much to do with the consequences of court intrigue for, despite a life marked by royal favor, Wyatt found himself on at least two occasions perhaps capriciously in royal disfavor and imprisoned in the Tower.

Baldi goes on to indicate, moreover, that, if unable to free himself from love, Wyatt cannot resort to a spiritual consolation:

For him the sufferings of love have no potential spiritual value; they are only a tax or penalty which he would be content to pay, however high, if he were sure of having the reward that should justly follow. Nor does he acknowledge the irrational nature of love; instead, he appears to be convinced that long service deserves to have "of right" its fitting recompense, the love of the lady. . . . In consequence, when the recompense or reward is not forthcoming, he follows Serafino Aquilano in calling on the woods, the mountains, the valleys and rivers to witness his wrongs. He throws the blame on the lady; hopes and believes that she will be punished by meeting with an equal unhappiness; and accuses Love of having a particular aversion for him.

This failure seems to be the cost of his having chosen to live only in the active world of politics. Cardinal Wolsey's advice about the "wretchedness" of the "man that hangs on princes' favours" may well have profited all Henry's counselors.

Lever has carefully traced the advances of Wyatt toward a more complex art form with his experiments in translating Petrarch, but, whatever innovations Wyatt and Skelton made toward humanizing the lyric, it remained to Surrey (1517–1547) to complete the process of the form's worldly descent by implicitly believing only in the literal level of its experience. In this belief, he antedates the scientism of the next century which saw the world as real and not some metaphoric journey toward a greater reality. Certainly, as Evans points out, Surrey created a revolution in poetry by having "pulled verse out of the medieval into the modern world." But the question of whether he or another "banished the aureate and alliterative once and for all, and established a standard of clear and controlled language" pales before his greater and more successful abandonment of the Augustinian *res-verba* distinctions of a moral world for the descriptive detail of a natural one. In this, one might argue, he is the father of the modern English landscape poem and a forerunner of Tennyson.

Unquestionably, of the three poets, Surrey comes closest in his lyrics to the depthless "speaking pictures" of Horace and the consequent "decorative" lyrics alternately praised and dismissed by later critics. Even in his translations of Petrarch, as Evans notes, "Surrey for the most part avoids Petrarchan sonnets with any concentration of thought and prefers to imitate those consisting of straight description. This is in part a reflection of his own personal interests; he had a feeling for nature and a power of natural description which is unique among the poets of his age." Of his love poetry, in *English Literature in the Sixteenth Century* Lewis remarks, it "is usually best when it is least about love. He takes every opportunity of bringing in external nature, or narrative, as if to take a holiday from the erotic treadmill. Oddly enough, the only two poems in which we are really moved by the theme of love are both put into the mouth of a woman; and of these women one certainly is, and the other may be, a wife in love with her husband."

Surrey, too, comes closest of the three to the rhetoric of narration and the logical framework which the Italian Renaissance critics were establishing for the lyric and which the importation of Petrarch demanded. "When Raging Love," for example, eschews the repetitions of the lyric song structure for the linear development of argument. Thus, rather than having a mood repeated in each stanza, as one might expect, it begins with a statement of condition ("when"), which in the second stanza moves to resultant action ("I call to mind") that extends into a third stanza and then flows into a fourth where the thoughts conclude ("Then think I thus"), thereupon to prompt in the last stanza the setting upon life action ("Therefore"). Clearly, years before Ramist logic, here is the process of the Aristotelian enthymeme at work. But more immediate and relevant is Surrey's reaffirming, particularly in the decorative effect of his love lyrics, the intermediate stage of courtly behavior and its conventional native system as the model of ethical Tudor court behavior.

# CHAPTER THREE

# Toward Originality

✿ The appearance in Italy of Petrarch is usually cited by historians who believe in a Renaissance as the beginning of the end of medievalism. His reverence for antiquity, his shunning of medieval theologians except St. Bernard, and his admiration of Cicero's Latin to the point of studied imitation provided the basis of a humanist tradition which to them signals the new age. In the fifteenth century, the growing impact of this tradition with its ornate rhetoric led first in Italy, then in France, and subsequently in England to conflicts with the *res-verba* relationships of the prevailing Augustinian "mixed" rhetoric. In so doing, it established for Renaissance literature clearly delineated concepts of imagination and originality. These concepts, in turn, influenced the creation of both Neo-Latin and vulgate literatures and, along with the changes in music theory which came in during the sixteenth century, greatly affected the English lyric after 1570. They help explain why, for example, Sidney holds a unique role among his contemporaries both as a model for English poets and as an original voice, and, at the same time, appears to Lee and subsequent critics as seriously indebted to Petrarch and Ronsard. "His habit," Lee points out, "was to paraphrase and adapt foreign writings rather than literally translate them. But hardly any of his poetic ideas, and few of his 'swelling phrases,' are primarily of his invention."

Source critics have shown how really few of the ideas and phrases in *Astrophel and Stella* are Sidney's own and have inferred that his contemporaries, who in many cases were adapting from the same sources, may not have known his indebtedness and, knowing, certainly would have objected to his claim of having looked into his heart and written. Other critics, disarmed by Sidney's indebtedness in these areas, have tried to suggest a kind of originality which is simply not there. As Izora Scott indicates in *Controversies over the Imitation of Cicero,* the nature of the conflicts and resultant concepts of imitation and originality which help to clarify the matter of Sidney's contemporary reputation derive much from the two schools of Ciceronianism which emerged in Italy after Petrarch's death.

These schools of Ciceronianism proposed to follow either the letter or the spirit of the master. In doing so, they wrapped a new stringency around the already partial acceptance of Cicero by St. Ambrose and St. Jerome, who had imitated his style and established the importance of Cicero for the teaching of rhetoric in the Middle Ages. The most influential properties of this new Ciceronianism did not emerge until after a shift in the *res-verba* relationships of *De doctrina Christiana* was accomplished. The balance of "delight" and "instruction" was upset toward a primacy of "delight." This shift toward form rather than matter may have been part of the humanists' already mentioned encroachments upon the speculative disciplines, for reflective of an underlying catholicity, the shift seems to have occurred regardless of which school of Ciceronianism a writer selected. For the lyric, as Thomas Bergin states in his Introduction to *Lyric Poetry of the Italian Renaissance,* there might have been an added impetus to this stress on style in the poet's having to discover the "illustrious" nature of the vernacular. "The Italian interest in words for words' sake and the obsession with technique," he explains, may owe "much to the Provençal masters who, as the first modern poets, must perforce have begun with such attitudes."

Certainly this care with the vernacular worked backward toward a new care for the Latin which was being used. Aided by the recovery of the complete texts of Cicero's *De oratore* and Quintilian's *Institutio oratorio* by 1422, one school of Latinists sought to achieve "delight" by limiting composition to the vocabulary, phrases, and forms of Cicero's own works as an absolute of "correct" style in eloquence. At Padua and at Florence, in the first half of the fifteenth century, this literalist school could list among its membership such early, influential humanists as Leonardo Bruni, Guarino da Verona, Giorgio da Trebisoda, Francesco Filelfo, Antonio Panormita, Aeneas Sylvius, and Ambrogio Traversari. The perfect type and probably the most influential member of the school was Gasparino Barzizza, who both lectured at the universities and earned the honor among early humanists of being the only writer before 1440 to attain "correct" style. A second, opposing, revisionist school was already implicit by the mid-fifteenth century in the writings of humanist Lorenzo Valla. Valla contended with Poggio Bacciolini that one could imitate Cicero very effectively by following the style of Quintilian. Poggio insisted that Cicero be the "correct" stylist's only model. This "liberalizing" view of Valla was followed by the views of Angelo Poliziano, who by 1490 defended his peculiar style against attacks by Bartolomeo Scala and Paolo Cortesi by appealing to the "spirit" of Ciceronian style. Politian denounced the superstitious "apes of Cicero" and urged originality. Like Poggio, Cortesi argued first for the acceptance of a model for correct style, and, then, for Cicero as that model.

By the sixteenth century, the revisionists could see that Padua, the home of the *humanitas* of the early fifteenth century, had declined into a seat of *servilitas,* controlled by Pietro Cardinal Bembo, Giacomo Sadoleto, Christophe de Longueil, and Simon de Villeneuve. At Rome, these revisionists pictured a society of *literati* under Bembo's protection, so exclusive that they bound themselves by oath to use no word except such as could be found in the works of Cicero. Accordingly, Bembo was supposed to have enlisted from Longueil the vow to read nothing but Cicero for five years and to have ordered Sadoleto to refrain from reading the Epistles of St. Paul on the grounds that they would contaminate his style. In 1512, Gianfrancesco Pico, a Florentine, sought to defend the position of the revisionists in an exchange of letters with Bembo. In 1528, Erasmus repeated the attack on the literal Ciceronians and imitation with his *Ciceronianus*. This Dialogue was followed by attacks in the 1540's by Peter Ramus, who in *Brutinae quaestiones in oratorem Ciceronis* (1547) attacked Cicero and in *Rhetoricae distinctiones in Quintilianum* (1549) attacked Quintilian.

Of these, the most important was Erasmus' attack, which resembles in theme the discussions that Pico presented to Bembo. It put forth the arguments which later critics would use for imitation in the vernacular and, as a major attack on the literalists, solicited their major replies. In it, Erasmus sought not to underestimate the value of Cicero as a master of style, but to question the Ciceronians' conception of imitation. He scoffed at a notion of "purity of style" and insisted that any reputable Latin was standard. In the manner of Augustine, he also insisted that matter (instruction) was more important than form (delight). Like Politian, he saw no greatness coming from a slavish imitation of another writer and wished style to accord with the writer's natural bent of genius. The Dialogue was answered by a then unknown physician-scholar, Julius Caesar Scaliger. Scaliger's two "Orations on Behalf of Cicero against Erasmus" (1529, 1536) answered in particular the charge "that imitation of Cicero did injury to letters and to young Christians" by declaring that letters, on the contrary, were saved from destruction by the "monuments" of Ciceronians, and, in echo of Augustine's compromise, that many Christians by the imitation of Cicero

77

had pleaded causes more eloquently. To Erasmus' charge that all could not hope to be successful imitators of Cicero because all could not succeed in lines which did not accord with their natural bents of genius, Scaliger answered, "Cicero was not perfect at birth. He became what he was by dint of work and development. An infinite number of Ciceros can be born and an infinite number of geniuses like his." Etienne Dolet, likewise, published a reply to Erasmus, *Dialogue in Behalf of Longueil against Erasmus* (1535). In it, he uses the figure of Erasmus' friend, the Englishman More, to present the Erasmanian arguments. The substance of Dolet's attack on the relevant points of imitation and originality differs little from that of Scaliger's.

During the Reformation these conflicts took on new coloring. The image of prelates poring over their volumes of Cicero rather than their Church Fathers was used by many reformers to illustrate the low state to which the Christian Church had fallen. Although the charges, made, according to Kristeller, "by hostile or narrow-minded contemporaries," should not be taken at face value or as a purely Protestant campaign, one should not discount their effects upon the popular imagination. In England, where even before the Reformation there had been anticlericism springing from dislike of the Church's coercive jurisdiction, its monetary exactions, and the unexemplary lives of its clergy, variations of Roger Ascham's picture in *The Schoolmaster* (1570) of harmful books "made in monasteries, by idle monks or wanton canons" must have been often repeated in sermons. In lean times, such depictions of prelates leading dissolute lives, in emulation of the very pagans whom the Church Fathers attacked, would have proved very inciting.

Yet, however much substance the conflicts over "correct" Latin style gave to the Reformation, they were intended mainly to settle matters of imitation and originality. In principle, their settlement differs little from the theories of imitation and originality presented by Roman writers. Both seem to agree that "one copies what one approves," that this copying, as in the case of the *Aeneid,* is not a source of disapprobation, that the subject matter for literature is generally *publica materies,* that in manner one treats an old subject "as no one else could," and finally that innovation, especially in subject matter, is dangerous. As Harold White indicates in *Plagiarism and Imitation during the English Renaissance,* these principles were carried over into the vernacular by critics generally before 1558. As pronounced by Leonard Cox's *The Art or Craft of Rhetoric* (1530), the principles could be as restrictive as anything proposed by the ardent literalists or, as proposed in Thomas Wilson's *The Art of Rhetoric* (1553), less servile.

The differences between Renaissance and classical theorists lay mainly in the insistence of writers like Cox that no originality whatever be permitted, and in the contentiousness, clarity, and rigidity that characterize both sides of the dispute. Two points, moreover, remained unsettled—the degree of selection, reinterpretation, and improvement that a writer must make before his work might be called original, and the status of an adaptation from another tongue which introduced a new genre into a language. The Roman theorists had allowed an adaptation of a Greek work to be considered "new" if, as in the case of Lucretius, the adaptation resulted in a new Latin genre. The Renaissance had not. As a consequence, many literalists found themselves dismissed as "Aesop's crows," sporting the feathers of another, for not having sufficiently assimilated their borrowings; and, in George Puttenham's *The Arte of English Poesie* (1589), John Southern is denied his boasted role of "originator" for having gone to Ronsard's French rather than to the Greek for his hymns of Pindar, Anacreontic odes, and other Greek lyrics.

By the mid-sixteenth century, these controversies over imitation had in England channeled themselves into four approved methods. Having established a model of style, a writer could imitate the model in the model's own tongue by servilely restricting himself to the model's principles, diction, images, and vocabulary; or by spiritually restricting himself to the model's principles, though not necessarily to the model's exact diction, images, and vocabulary, but to diction, images, and vocabulary which are suited to the writer's own personality by the writer's having extended the principles of his model to the range of other reputable writers; or a writer could imitate the model in the writer's language by servilely restricting himself to an approximation of the model's principles, diction, imagery, and vocabulary; or by spiritually restricting himself to the model's principles, though not necessarily to an approximation of the model's exact limitations of diction, imagery, and vocabulary, but to an approximation of diction, images, and vocabulary suited to the writer's own personality, again by extending the range of his model to include other reputable writers. In short, in a matter like the imitation of Petrarch, a writer might imitate Petrarch either by restricting himself to Petrarch's Italian or by extending it to include the language of other reputable Italian writers, or by restricting himself to literal translations of Petrarch into suitable English, or finally by approximating in suitable English the effects of Petrarch. Moreover, as Tillyard states in *The Poetry of Sir Thomas Wyatt,* "if it was patriotic to write well in the English tongue, it was doubly patriotic to write in an Italian or French form, to show that an English poet could compete with the foreigner on his own ground."

The key to all these methods of imitation is the word "model," which conveys a working toward something. A writer's success depended upon his sounding like his model, not, as critics seem to suggest, by his sounding like himself. *The Book of the Courtier, The Schoolmaster,* and Gabriel Harvey's *Ciceronianus* and *Rhetor* (1577) all advocate models. Their authors varied only in the emphases which they placed upon the classical safeguards of originality. In the lyric, purists clearly demanded imitation of Petrarch either in Italian or in English adaptations adjusted to the style of Chaucer. With such demands, Wyatt's use of the "broken-back" line to echo Chaucerian rhythms seems less eccentric, as do Harvey's branding of Chaucer's Troilus as "Astrophel's cordial" and Ascham's attack on poets who fail in these demands: "Some that make *Chaucer* in English and *Petrarch* in Italian their gods in verses, and yet be not able to make true difference, what is a fault and what is just praise in those two worthy wits, will much mislike this my writing. But such men be even like followers of *Chaucer* and *Petrarch,* as one here in England did follow Sir *Thomas More,* who, being most unlike unto him in wit and learning, nevertheless in wearing his gown awry upon one shoulder, as Sir *Thomas More* was wont to do, would needs be counted like unto him."

However severe the strictures against originality seem among professional writers, the doctrine of imitation and its application were even narrower in the schools which the new generation of writers attended. Despite the controversies in which the spiritual Ciceronians pleaded for a lessening of exact imitation, most of the treatises on rhetoric used in schools followed slavishly the ideas of Cicero and Quintilian. The treatises did so regardless of what their authors professed elsewhere on the matters of "delight" and "instruction" and, on occasion, conflicted with these statements. The "German Cicero" Johann Sturm and his educational theory influenced most of these treatises. Under his theory, the prevailing method of learning good style was the making of notebooks in which were copied Ciceronian words and phrases and quotations to be memorized and used in composition. In England, Dean Colet's School of St. Paul, while otherwise following the Sturm curriculum, excluded pagan authors and substituted in their stead Ciceronian Church Fathers. Ascham would allow for pagan writers, but only if they were taught coevally with the Bible: "As Plato and Aristotle in

Greek, Tully in Latin, be so either wholly or sufficiently left unto us, as I never knew yet scholar that gave himself to like, and love, and follow chiefly those three authors, but he proved both learned, wise, and also an honest man, if he joined with all the true doctrine of God's Holy Bible, without which the other three be but fine-edge tools in a fool or a mad-man's hand." In this way, "delight" could be tempered with "instruction." Still, Ascham is enough of an admirer of Sturm to have written to him about his pupil, Princess Elizabeth, that besides "her conversational ability in French, Italian, English, Latin and Greek, and her delight and skill in music," she had "a gift for perceiving what makes literary style good or bad." Under his tutelage, she had spent long hours in reading Cicero.

Opposed to these restricting doctrines which might have made imitation a stultifying, superstitious ritual were forces that would turn both music and poetry in new directions. The major of these forces was the individualism that historians since 1860 have seen as one aspect of the period. In *The Civilization of the Renaissance in Italy,* Jacob Burckhardt establishes the direction: "Man [in the Middle Ages] was conscious of himself only as a member of a race, people, party, family, or corporation— only through some general category. In Italy this veil first melted into air; an *objective* treatment and consideration of the State and of all the things of this world became possible. The *subjective* side at the same time asserted itself with corresponding emphasis; man became a spiritual *individual,* and recognized himself as such. . . . The ban laid upon human personality was dissolved; and a thousand figures meet us each in its own special shape and dress." More recently Kristeller has reaffirmed as a characteristic feature of the Renaissance this "tendency to express, and to consider worth expressing, the concrete uniqueness of one's feelings, opinions, experiences, and surroundings, a tendency which appears in the biographical and descriptive literature of the time as well as in the portrait painting, which is present in all the writings of the humanists, and which finds its fullest philosophical expression in Montaigne, who claims that his own self is the main subject matter of his philosophy." Even Charles Homer Haskins, who in *The Renaissance of the Twelfth Century* holds out for an earlier revival, concedes "that the twelfth century lacks the wealth and variety of the striking personalities in which the Italian Renaissance abounds. It has no such mass of memoirs and correspondence, its outstanding individuals are relatively few. Nor can it claim the artistic interest of portraiture. Its art is rich and distinctive both in sculpture and architecture, but it is an art of types, not of individuals. It has left us no portraits of scholars or men of letters, very few even of rulers or prelates."

The veil of collectivism, which Burckhardt speaks of as having begun to lift in Italy in the thirteenth century, lifted in England in the sixteenth century, and, although as Douglas Bush indicates in *The Renaissance and English Humanism,* the view of "rebellious individualism is much too simple and exclusive," nevertheless, the idea of individualism creates a new literary genre and begins to alter both music and lyric theory. Independently in the minds of Jerome Cardan, a physician, Benvenuto Cellini, an artist, and Thomas Whythorne, a composer, the impulse for a sustained public self-examination emerges, and autobiographical elements increasingly intrude into the literature; for with idea of individualism, the development of self-consciousness of which individualism is a manifestation becomes established. According to Ernst Cassirer's *The Individual and the Cosmos in Renaissance Philosophy*, this development of self-consciousness consists in the Renaissance thinker's ability to view himself "in perspective" as an object in a manner similar to Erwin Panofsky's description in *Studies in Iconology* of the Renaissance thinker's new ability to view the past as a separate entity: "No medieval man could see the civilization of antiquity as a phenomenon complete in itself, yet belonging to the past and historically detached from the contemporary world,—as a cultural cosmos to be investigated and, if possible, to be reintegrated, instead of being a world of living wonders or a mine of information."

This development in consciousness owes much to the work of the philosopher Marsilio Ficino, which, following the mystical literature of the Middle Ages, continued to bind knowledge and love. For Ficino, the act of knowledge, having like the act of love the goal of overcoming the separation in the elements of being and returning them to the point of their original unity, became identified in its highest intellection with "a thinking consciousness." By means of love, this "consciousness" moved the mind to divide itself into two and to confront itself with a world of objects of knowledge as objects of contemplation. "But," according to Cassirer, "the act of knowledge that initiates this division, this sacrifice of the original unity for multiplicity, is also capable of *overcoming* it. For to know an object means to negate the distance between it and consciousness; it means, in a certain sense, to become *one* with the object." Thus in 1575, the physician Cardan in *De vita propria liber,* at the end of his lifetime and in order to know himself, sat down to analyze himself as if he were one of his patients.

Still, if Ficino defined self-consciousness in philosophical terms, *Il cortegiano* developed its practical, social aspects. The book established itself as a normative educational guide to make man aware, first, of a wide range of human possibilities and activities, and, then, of a harmony of thought and action, learning and feeling, which he might achieve by imposing on them a common lifestyle. This style remains a unique human possibility because only man brings together into a single consciousness contradictory impulses and disparate, fragmented experiences, and only he can impose those relationships, rhythms, accents, and symmetries on experience that are the very requisites of style. As men may turn the contents of consciousness into works of art, so may they manage themselves into works of art. Ficino recognizes this possibility when he sees the task of the artist as resembling that of love—the joining of things that are separate and opposed. The artist seeks the "invisible" in the "visible," the "intelligible" in the "sensible." Although his intuition and his art are determined by his vision of the pure form, he can possess this pure form only if he succeeds in realizing it in matter; so, too, with one's consciousness of oneself.

Yet neither Ficino nor Castiglione would have had so great an effect if despotism and Protestantism had not fostered the cultivation of inward resources. Under despots, as Burckhardt suggests, "These people were forced to know all the inward resources of their own nature, passing and permanent; and their enjoyment of life was enhanced and concentrated by the desire to obtain the greatest satisfaction from a possibly very brief period of power and influence." Nor, as James M. Osborn cautions in his Introduction to *The Autobiography of Thomas Whythorne,* should one suppose this despotism restricted itself to Italy. This tyranny was also true of the Tudor monarchs, "all of whom could have been nicknamed 'Bloody,' though the epithet stuck only to Catholic Mary." "Proper and prudent conduct was an everyday problem, for the consequences of transgression, whether from one's fellow man or God's wrath, ever impended." Moreover, a reading of any of the major Reform theologians makes clear the stress of Protestantism upon the individual rather than the congregation, particularly in matters of prayer.

For the writer, as for Montaigne in 1580, the impulse of "self" must have offered new, anticontemplative subject matter. By choosing to write of himself instead of his learning, he put an importance upon his active nature that coincided with the active disposition of the period. Still, as Harry Alpert indicates in *Emile Durkheim and His Sociology,* the concepts of individualism are complex in a single writer, let alone in an entire century. Alpert finds at least five contexts for the word in Durkheim's writing: the biological entity, the psychological entity, the isolated person (viewed as if he lived in total physical and mental isolation), the social person (as he is made by others and by himself to appear in their experiences and his own in the course of social relations), and the "real" individual (as a member of society and as a complete personality). For Renaissance writers and historians, an individual was a biological and religious entity rather than a psychological one. Individual writers and works, however, shifted from the isolated to the social personality, and, at times, also incorporated a "real" individual. In "Individualism as a Criterion of the Renaissance," Norman Nelson finds that this vacillation is a main cause of disagreement among historians.

Moreover, despite Bush's argument that the problem of individualism may not have been new in the literature or in the philosophy since elements of it have existed in all great literature, the position it occupies in the concept of originality as well as in the literature of the sixteenth century is so similar to the accomplishment of Masaccio, who according to Giorgio Vasari is to be granted the origination of "drapery with few folds and an easy fall as they are in natural life," that it cannot be handled traditionally. This is not that Masaccio invented the drapery of clothes, but that he was able to make it viable subject matter for art, and what is going on in the arts is that the sustained self is made viable subject matter.

In the realm of autobiography, this subject matter went into structures immediately seized from scientific, fictional, religious, and historical forms, depending upon the form with which the writer sought to associate his life's meaning. In addition, since autobiography is a narrative or history, what the writer during the Renasisance often saw as himself was what he was able to accept as true of all men —the scholastic "predicables"—as well as what he was able to divorce from a central intelligence. The "persona" which resulted was clearly never quite the actual man, although one feels a sense of humanity. Depending upon the meaning of life which the writer selected, the abstraction took the direction either of objective detail, resembling a chronicle (the social person), or of subjective history, resembling Augustine's *Confessions* (the isolated person). In either case, the abstraction relied upon certain established techniques. It chose a clear point in space-time from which to merge present (character definition) and past (character history); moreover, as Wayne Shumaker indicates in *English Autobiography,* compared to the abstractions of biography, it tended to show subjects more passive to their environments, readier to react to stimuli, less prone to initiate deeds of their own volition, and more given to rumination. Characteristically, it tended to exclude social bearing, voice, idiosyncratic gestures, and odd mannerisms of which the writer remained ignorant, although indirectly some qualities came through. In the case of English autobiography, as Anna Robeson Burr relates in *The Autobiography,* "The literature . . . is full of atmosphere and objective detail. The rural life . . . [is painted] as if it were the stage-setting of a drama. Nor is it true of the countryside alone." She opposes this depiction to that of the French, whose "minds are turned inward upon personalities" and towards the *"aspect conscient."*

In music theory, this individualism took on several distinct characteristics as music moved to its new humanistic role through new kinds of patronage, new values in musical notes, and changes in the hierarchy of song with the widespread acceptance of unaccompanied instrumental music. First, the concepts of words and music and of *musica mundana* underwent serious alterations. Treatises where words and music could not be separated by memory gave way to those where music theory entered what Stevens calls its "utilitarian" and "abstract" stages. Seay has placed this entrance well into the fourteenth century, when "overwhelming fascination with technical novelties" replaced speculative interests. But now Ficino gives substance to the changes in attitude in his "De divino furore." In this work, he images the human soul receiving through the ears a memory of that divine music which is found first in the mind of God and second in the order and movement of the heavens. This memory precipitates imitations of divine music by means of voice and instruments, and high imitation through serious music and poetry by means of verse and meter. In these delineations, he is still close to Augustine and Boethius, with one notable change. Ficino has lyric and score independently affect different human qualities. The lyric aims at man's rationality and the score at man's passions, so that, despite his view of music as a means of expelling the disturbances of the body and soul and of uplifting man's mind toward God and intelligible things, a division is set up comparable to the division between logic and rhetoric wherein the closed fist of lyric (logic) relates to the open palm of score (rhetoric).

Indicative of the roles established by the division are a reinterpretation of music's healing powers along worldly rather than unworldly lines and an increasing sense that music's embellishment of words could be approximated with rhetorical analogues. Sixteenth-century medical compendiums record that music "doth appease the dolours of the mind," and even so skeptical a person as Elyot, who in *The Governor* (1531) inveighs against music, is willing in *Castle of Health* (1539) to allow its medical application. The rhetorical analogues reflect a parallel shift from symbolic to symptomatic concerns. They seem to convey a new attempt to identify the recently seen persuasive rather than the illustrative powers of score with the traditional persuasive powers of rhetoric. In "Music and Learning in the Early Italian Renaissance," Kristeller tries to make the analogues wholly dependent upon humanism, finding them consistent with the origins of humanism as a literary and rhetorical movement, whose major concern was the study, imitation, and revival of ancient eloquence and learning after a long period of neglect. He points out that the humanist contribution "consisted mostly in greater eloquence of style, in a new emphasis on ancient source materials, in the claim of a rebirth of the subject after a time of decline, and finally in various attempts to restore certain forms of ancient doctrine or practice." He mentions that as early as 1492 Ficino listed music among the arts and sciences "revived" in his time.

The "revival" of ancient practices, as E. E. Lowinsky conjectures in *Secret Chromatic Art in the Netherlands Motet,* led to the creation of a *musica reservata* and changes in the style of motet music around 1550 that coincided with changes in the concept of the nature of music as a whole. "The avowed aim," he states, "of the *musica reservata* was *rem quasi actam ante oculos ponere.*" This new goal of presenting an event in such a way that the listener sees it before his very eyes, as in a dramatic performance, separates the older religious style of Nicholas Gombert from that of his successor, Orlando Lasso. Some time before the impact of Netherlands music upon English music, as Adrianus Petit Coclico seems to signify in his *Compendium musices* (1552), *musica reservata* "removes music from its traditional place in the *quadrivium,* from its union with mathematical order and the harmony of the spheres, and associates it with the *trivium* consisting of grammar, dialectics, and rhetoric, or, in other words, with the human world and its main vehicle of communication, human speech." The concept of *musica reservata,* in addition, seems to have motivated Nicolo Vicentino's attempt to revive the enharmonic and chromatic genera of ancient music in *L'antica musica ridotta alla moderna practica* (1555). There, as Lowinsky notes, evidence becomes even stronger for *musica reservata*'s having "to do primarily with a style of composition, at whose center stood the intimate union of word and music and with it the transition from a purely melodic-melismatic style to a syllabic-declamatory." Thus Hollander's contention is borne out, that if music was to be made "to conform to its image in the mythology of Antiquity, its very structural devices and building blocks" had to be redefined so as to "be seen as operating directly upon the feelings of its auditors, rather than as merely serving the more idealized and abstract interests of organic structure."

The attitudes toward music during the Reformation reinforced these changes by denying to music its transcendental quality. In his *Disputation on Gregorian Chant* (1521), Andreas Bodenstein von Karlstadt argued that chant put "distance between the mind and God." Given its "high order" of imitation, a singer must concentrate even more intently upon the music so that by necessity he must be first a musician and second a human being at prayer. This applied equally for the accompanist. Karlstadt concluded that all instruments should be banished from worship and proposed that instead the whole congregation should sing psalms in the vernacular. The result of his *Disputation* was a reduction of the range of language (*verba*) from Gregory's extensions of it to both statuary and music. Other Reformation critics followed Karlstadt in his attack. They proceeded usually along three lines. First, liturgical music was not explicitly commanded by God in either the Old or New Testament. Second, Christ instructed men to pray to God individually and in private; and, last, St. Paul urged men, when together, to worship God and pray to him in their hearts. As Charles Garside, Jr., has shown in *Zwingli and the Arts,* "Music for Zwingli thus exists without the additional theological dimension given to it by Luther and Calvin; it is merely an art which for a little time is immensely affecting emotionally. And to music Zwingli will not accord the sanction of the Paraclete; he considered it, on the contrary, wholly secular." In *Protestantism and Progress,* Ernst Troeltsch remarks that Protestantism in general "never elevated artistic feeling into the principle of a philosophy of life, of metaphysics or ethics. It could not do that, because its asceticism and its absolute metaphysical dualism made it impossible."

Through Nicholas Ridley many of Zwingli's ideas got to England, and Roland Bainton in *The Reformation of the Sixteenth Century* describes the progress of the Anglican communion as marked by Lutheran leanings under the protectorate of Somerset and by Zwinglian and Calvinist tendencies under that of Northumberland. Some of the changes in the second version of the Book of Common Prayer (1552) can be attributed to this Zwinglian influence. By the 1570's, Whythorne notes, two schools of religious musicians evolved, reflective of the divided communion—the "speculators" under the new dispensation, who became "musicians by study, without any practice thereof [in their hearts]," and those under the old dispensation, who in the practice of music "either set forth God's glory in the church, or else use it for the same purpose in private houses, or else for their own recreation," but who do not make their livelihood at it. He records the general waning of the latter: "First, for the Church, ye do and shall see it so slenderly maintained in the cathedral churches and colleges and parish churches, that when the old store of musicians be worn out, the which were bred when the music of the church was maintained (which is like to be in short time), ye shall have few or none remaining, except it be a few singingmen and players on musical instruments." In *Music and the Reformation in England 1549–1660,* Peter LeHuray provides the statistics of this decline. Boyd also cites the decline, noting that most of the song schools were discontinued when Edward VI confiscated the chantries and, despite a brief period of revival under Mary, continued to decline under Elizabeth when in most English schools music was replaced in the curriculum by arithmetic. Of the writers on education, only Richard Mulcaster in his treatises champions music wholeheartedly. Moreover, in most of the places where one would expect a flourishing body of music which might effect either the *musica mundana* or the *musica humana*—cathedrals, private chapels, private houses—full-time musicians gave way to "off-scum" minstrels, who, according to Whythorne, offered their services like common beggars "to every Jack, going about every place and country." Nor was this decline true of England alone. Its pervasiveness affirms perhaps more the chamber, rather than church, direction of the *musica reservata.*

The effect upon musical style which the restrictions upon *musica mundana* and *musica humana* and the new emphasis on rhetoric produced is clear. Popular tendencies toward individualistic expression accelerated. In religious music, LeHuray sees in the search for simple and comprehensive musical style "a gradual shift from 'successive' to 'simultaneous' techniques of composition—from a primarily horizontal method of working, in which the separate parts were composed one after the other, to a vertical method in which all parts were developed simultaneously." This shift from diachronic to synchronic composition permitted music to become more representative and expressive, and composers, more individualistic. Previously the anonymity of the *musica mundana,* like the objectivity of mathematics, intruded to make the composer speak for Christendom through objectified, transpersonal reflections on God. Now, appropriate to the successive moments of music which the new technique of composition afforded, more attention could be accorded the rhetorical and programmatic qualities of the score. Sounds dissolved into sympathetic responses, so that arrangements became happy, sad, wistful, or heroic; and criticism, reflective of these dissolutions, began to assess the propriety of scores to human messages rather than to supposed contemplative encounters. No longer did functions classify music as dirge, festive, martial, or dance. Music became its happy, sad, wistful, or heroic responses. As LeHuray points out, "Very many of the earliest English anthems already reveal a preference for 'subjective' texts of clearly defined mood, and it is certainly wrong to think of the dramatic, subjective anthem text as a late-Elizabethan phenomenon. Similar changes are to be observed in the Latin music of the period."

In the realm of secular music, this growing individualism provided for what in *Music in the Renaissance* Gustave Reese cites as a "unique nationalization" of the Italian madrigal during the 1580's. "Never before," he notes, "and perhaps never afterward have English musicians adopted a foreign style with such whole-heartedness and intelligence, and at the same time added so much of their own and produced so distinguished a native repertory." As Joseph Kerman cautions in *The English Madrigal*, the precise extent of this individualism in English music is hard to determine, for, unlike their Italian counterparts, English composers seldom set different musical scores to the same lyrics. Yet their "unique nationalization," as E. H. Fellowes notes in *The English Madrigal Composers,* tended until about 1600 to be expressed in a subordination of growing instrumental interests to melodic line. Adding that unlike the music developed by Italian madrigalists, English music at this time did not attempt to illustrate meaning point by point, Kerman concludes: "The English song on the contrary is an abstract composition that obeys purely musical rather than literary dictates, and looks stylistically either to an ancient native tradition of strophic song, or to the established idioms of English church music, which are more Netherlandish than Italian in orientation." Still, the mere variety of musical manners offered to the English composer at this time permitted him to show his individuality simply in his choice of idiom. Two of England's best composers, William Byrd and Orlando Gibbons, could choose not to write madrigals without damage to their reputations.

In the case of the lyric, its having been placed among the logical discourses by Renaissance theorists like Varchi made it susceptible to logical techniques, and its having been relegated in many treatises to dealing with both the Aristotelian example and the enthymeme permitted it to take its significance, not only from the scholastic "predicables," but from the more individualistic scholastic "predicaments" as well. As Thomas Wilson notes in his *Rule of Reason* (1551), the difference between the predicaments (general words) and predicables (common words) is that "the Predicables set forth the largeness of words," whereas "the Predicaments do name the very nature of things, declaring (and that substantially) what they are in very deed." The placement of the lyric among these techniques permitted the poet to take man out of his definition as "a living creature endowed with reason, having aptness by nature to speak" and to put the stress upon man's accidents or categories, and with the change, alter the very form of the lyric toward a false discipline relying upon its own system of probabilities for its validity.

The precedent for the change to predicaments is at least as old as Aristotle, who in his *Rhetoric,* when discussing "benevolence," indicates that "we must examine [a given act] under all the Categories; for an act is benevolent either in being a particular thing, or in having a particular magnitude, or in having a particular quality, or in occurring at a particular time, or in a particular place." Moreover, the shift to Ramist logic which occurred principally during the 1570's gave new importance to these predicaments as arguments in themselves and not simply as tools for argumentation. As Rosemund Tuve indicates, "The Ramistic notion of figures in a discourse—that they are 'arguments'—contributed, as usual, nothing but an emphasis." This "emphasis" asserts that "to see something in one of the predicaments, in whatever type of discourse, is to argue something." She concludes, in justifying the increased logicality in the handling of imagery, "One does not thereafter need to be told that good poems are made by good logicians; and the logical complexity and conceptually functional use of the metaphysical image begin to seem like the norm toward which all images should strive." Thus, although there were no changes in the concept of man as a creature of body and soul, there were apparently changes in the weight given to the conditions affecting that concept that allowed for the expression of individualism. Such emphasis centered on those properties of mind and body to which some tag might be given, as from the possession of wisdom, one might be called wise, or from the doing of justice, one might be called just, and provided for the growing new norm of Elizabethan verse.

In writing, the depiction of these properties involved the acceptance of an anti-Averroistic view that no intellectual function can conceivably exist dissociated from the realm of sensible material. "To become effective the mind requires a body corresponding and 'adequate' to it." As Nicholas Cusanus expresses it, between the body and soul there exists not only a relationship of connection but also of complete "concinnity," of continuous proportion: "The vision of *your* eye cannot be the vision of any other eye, even if it could be detached from your eye and connected to the eye of another, for it would not find in the other eye the measure it had in yours.—And the power of

99

distinction in *your* vision cannot be the power of distinction in someone else's vision. So, too, *one* intellect cannot think in all men." Cassirer has already dealt with the prevalence of Cusanus' notions in Italy in the early Renaissance. Paul H. Kocher in *Science and Religion in Elizabethan England* discusses this same "concinnity" between body and soul as it affects Elizabethan medicine: "It was Elizabethan medical recognition that states of soul are inevitably reflected in the matter which the soul inhabits." Except for will, the body generally determined all man's actions. In "Physiology and Psychology in Shakespeare's Age," Patrick Cruttwell shows Shakespeare's acceptance of the belief that "one's ideas on man's body were connected with ideas on his soul and character, on his actions as a political animal, and on the universe," thus showing the widespread circulation of "concinnity" despite Church attempts to contain it. Sir John Davies' "Nosce Teipsum" represents the opposite, more conservative Church view of an "influence" rather than "concinnity."

Under the beliefs of the day, these predicaments were thought to be acquired either by habit or by labor, and the exact determination of their acquisition contributed to recurrent controversies about the effects of Nature and Art on individual character. For example, in determining if nobility were inherited or a product of individual character, Castiglione went back to Aristotle's view that it was a personal virtue accompanied with inherited wealth. The best qualities, one soon discovered, were inherited and mental, for as one could produce a fine tree by breeding, so one could also produce a fine human being. But, as the century was an age of a rising middle class and of self-made men, allowances were made constantly for upgrading self-made properties. Within these predicaments, properties fell into four general groups: virtues, or qualities which affected the mind, derived mainly from the classical virtues of Prudence, Wisdom, Justice, Fortitude, and Temperance; powers, which affected both mind and body; passions, including affectations, which likewise affected both mind and body, but which did so by eliminating will; and the figure or body of an individual, which was wholly physical. In addition to these qualities, more attention was paid to the other Aristotelian categories of *relativa, actio, passio, quando, ubi, situs,* and *habitus.*

To illustrate how the use of these properties would affect English poetry, one need only take a look at Sidney's *Astrophel and Stella.* In the sequence he carefully lets his reader know, as part of the hero's delineation, where the action is, whether it is day or night, the hero's various posturings and dress, and his relations to others. In so doing, he creates for the first time in English lyric poetry, and as a consequence of predicaments, a persona who controls with recognizable voice and attitudes the whole sequence in the way that the lover of Laura governs Petrarch's *Canzonieri.* This persona, as David Kalstone suggests in *Sidney's Poetry,* emerges by Sidney's pitting the experiences of the sequence against the clear background of Petrarch: "Often things are quite different from what he [Astrophel] has been led to expect: he does not love at first sight (sonnet 2); he is impatient with attitudes his role imposes (sonnet 56: 'Fy schoole of Patience, Fy, your lesson is / Far far too long to learne it without booke')." This contrast permits a kind of mental *contentio*, equivalent to that which Wyatt uses in his songs and, in the interplay, manages to bring into tension both the Petrarchan and native love conventions. In this tension, although he inevitably sides against Petrarch, Sidney uses the circumstances (predicaments) to define the aptness of Astrophel's responses as well as to establish the manner of the importation of Petrarchism into England. Thus, however much Astrophel, for example, basks in Stella's purifying power, he still undergoes no religious transformation; likewise, however real his feelings are, they too often turn at court into affectations; in addition, his strivings toward a philosophy of love, as in the Petrarchan sonnet 71, are met repeatedly with rejection: "But ah," Desire still cries, "give me some food."

Kept at the level of defining the alterations which love (both power and passion) has produced in his hero's make-up, this contention contrasts the predominant qualities of passion or of power stressed mainly in an earlier view of poetry where the situation was left unlocalized or montonous. Wyatt's "autobiographical" sonnet, "The piller perisht," provides an excellent example of the earlier form. In it, according to Mason, Wyatt uses Petrarch similarly as a standard against which to establish in anti-Averroistic fashion his own individual measure of grief at the death of Thomas Cromwell. The imagery of the poem, however, is so generalized as to cast doubt upon the occasion and the location, and so consistent as to seem without tension. No clear-cut predicament establishes its subject as Cromwell, though there is no reason to question Mason's reading. The "piller" simply sits in the memory where objective measurement of space and time is impossible. So, too, does Anne Boleyn in "Whoso list to hunt." Wyatt again never really asserts the place she inhabits. His quest is identified only with an emblem of a necklace (presumably real) bearing a conventional inscription: *"Noli me tangere,* for Caesar's I am." The same doe, necklace, and inscription appear in Petrarch's sonnet 157. Predicaments simply are not utilized.

The very utilization of predicaments, which, as Charles Lamb pointed out in "Some Sonnets of Sir Philip Sydney" (1823), keeps Sidney's sequence from becoming vague and unlocalized, requires the use of two kinds of detail: one, to complete the persona; the other, to complete the poem. Thus, in *Astrophel and Stella,* one encounters lines and expressions whose primary function is to reveal something of the nature of Astrophel, and others whose primary function is to move the narrative forward. In the first instance, a great abundance of personal material is required; nor can it be random. As Kalstone remarks, even the conventional military images to describe love's conquest contribute: "They serve to characterize Astrophel as plain-speaking: with soldierly directness [in sonnet 2] he admits that Cupid's is not a 'dribble shot' and grudgingly recognizes conquest and enemy 'decrees.' Such details —along with the colloquial terseness of 'slave-borne *Muscovite'—*contribute to the tone of masculine reasonableness that marks Sidney's sonnets off from others."

Moreover, to everlasting scholarly chagrin, Sidney is not beyond supplying details from his own life to flesh out Astrophel. In the second instance, rapid shifts of place and mood occur to generate a sense of linear sequence. Both kinds of details are selected according to the principle of probability rather than by a practice of depicting accurately instants of emotion. This probability moves the form closer to Aristotelian tragedy and to the false disciplines of Renaissance criticism. Moreover, the combination of the two kinds of detail gives rise perhaps to a sequence of poems as the best form in which to collect and arrange these details. Certainly, one cannot fill out a character in the short lyric, although one could portray a generalized emotion or a single state of mind. Either because its melodies tended to make it brief or because its method of extension tended to make it strophic, musical structures prevented such creations. But a sequence does allow for the variety which establishes the ranges of character as well as the ranges of action. Moreover, the sense of justice which would result from the arrangement of the parts would make violence and sensuousness more possible, for, as in all "false" worlds, the sins committed within the world's frame are there meted justice. Some unpleasantnesses one can bear chiefly because one knows they will be solved before the work's completion.

By the 1580's these predicaments, which in literature led to a greater sense of life (*energia*), in criticism began to lead to a sharpening of the definition of originality that would obtain. Sidney, for one, in *An Apology for Poetry* (*c.* 1583) in stressing the spirit rather than the letter of imitation writes, "A poet no industry can make, if his own genius be not carried into it: and therefore is it an proverb, *Orator fit, Poeta nascitur.*" He condemns "the meaner sort of painters who counterfeit only such faces as are set before them" and praises the more excellent, "who, having no law but wit, bestow that in colors upon you which is fittest for the eye to see," and advises a Canidia who desires "to fashion her countenance to the best grace" to accept a painter's portrait of "a most sweet face, with Canidia written upon it" rather than a portrait as she is, "who, Horace sweareth, was foul and ill-favored." Still, as his dismissal of Spenser's *The Shepherd's Calendar* indicates, he is not for leaving authority altogether: "That same framing of his style to an old rustic language I dare not allow, since neither Theocritus . . . Virgil . . . nor Sanazar did affect it."

Recognizing the effect of Ciceronianism as essentially a loss of *energia,* he writes to his brother, "So you can speak and write Latin not barbarously I never require great study in Ciceronianism, the chief abuse of Oxford, [where] while following the words, they neglect the things themselves." Elsewhere in the *Apology,* he objects on similar grounds to servile Petrarchism. He writes that "so coldly they apply fiery speeches as men that had rather read lovers' writings, and so caught up certain swelling phrases . . . than that in truth they feel those passions." He reaffirms the objection in sonnets 1, 3, 6, 15, 74, and 90 of *Astrophel and Stella,* stating his case most clearly in 15:

> You that old *Petrarch's* long deceasèd woes
> With new-born sighs, and wit disguisèd sing;
> You take wrong ways, those far-fet helps be such,

As do bewray a want of inward touch,
And sure, at length, stol'n goods do come to light.

These calls for originality in the practice of imitation are asserted as well by King James VI of Scotland in *An Short Treatise* (1584), William Webbe in *A Discourse of English Poetry* (1586), Puttenham in *The Arte of English Poesie* (1589), and Harrington in a Preface to *Orlando Furioso* (1591). As White sums the matter up, all tend to uphold imitation, rightly understood, as not only proper but praiseworthy and even essential. All consider eclecticism in the choice of models a recognized literary principle and cite a wide variety of masters to be followed. "Reinterpretation and improvement of borrowed matter," White goes on to explain, "are demanded generally, with attacks on concealed borrowing and servile imitation. Subject matter is common property, and Sidney, James, and Puttenham are distrustful of individual fabrication, but somewhat less so than classical writers were. In short, White concludes, all are "in substantial agreement, not only with classical thought, but with their Renaissance predecessors and contemporaries on the Continent, as well as with their predecessors in England."

With their cries for originality based upon the idea of a singular "personality" or "genius" which could be abtracted from a work, what these critics are calling for is the creation of a particularly English sustained persona in literature to oppose both the anonymous pre-Petrarchan lyric poet and the unacceptable Petrarchan persona. As in rhetoric, this persona would evolve when the writer, aware of the persuasive nature of his task, would use his judgment to frame a mask—not necessarily a false one—that would present him at his best. In simple terms, the poet would choose those qualities of his personality which by pleasing would give him most assurance of success. Sidney notes the existence of this intention in his *Apology:* "But truly many of such writings as come under the banner of irresistable love, if I were a Mistress, would never persuade me they were in love." But, originality would also require, as Donne indicates in "An Anatomy of the World: the First Anniversary" (1611), an underlying philosophical singularity. Each man would, in fact, as Cusanus had posited, have "got / To be a phoenix, and that there can be / None of that kind, of which he is, but he." The methods of this singularity and sustained, acceptable persona, expressed by Astrophel's looking into his heart and writing, become to his contemporaries Sidney's genius and originality.

# CHAPTER FOUR

# New Alliances

To understand how the humanist shifts from medieval to renaissance concerns influenced the new alliances of the Elizabethan lyric, one should perhaps recall that in the pre-Petrarchan lyric, the listener was persuaded, convinced, deterred, exhorted, and generally moved, not by the singer, but by the instrument which the singer could with music and words evoke from the mystical *musica mundana*. This instrument, in turn, tuned in the listener. Song as such was aimed not toward communication with one's fellowman but toward some superhuman release and return. It fitted a system similar to that of Platonic love which Ficino's Commentary to the *Symposium* had developed late in the fifteenth century. Song in this new system required a connecting, transpersonal agent in addition to two human beings, as Ficino's lovers had needed God as their insoluble bond and perpetual guardian. Now, according to the aims of the new *musica reservata*, song was to present scenes before the eyes of the listener, and the

listener respond, as it were, directly to incidents con-
structed by his imagination out of what was believed to
be the illusions of reality that song transmitted. The
contemporary *Spiritual Exercises* of St. Ignatius and the
newly reinstituted *Rhetoric* of Aristotle provide corol-
laries for the response. Specifically the change meant that
score and words became discrete, active means of persu-
asion, literally the "instruments" of a conscious rhetorical
process, used in the religious song to invite participation
in incidents in the life of Christ and, in the erotic scheme,
to move a passive auditor-victim-beloved on a worldly
level. By making the singer responsible for moving himself
religiously in one and for moving his love in the other,
song thus interiorized and extended the areas under man's
control.

The result of these extensions and new responsibilities
was that music and words were forced to rely even more
heavily upon rhetorical devices, thus uniting the forms
more intimately with sixteenth-century treatises on rhet-
oric. In music, as early as Johannes Cochlaeus' *Tetrachor-
dium musices* (1511) and Pietro Aron's *Il Toscanello in
musica* (1523), theorists began to employ substructures of
rhetoric rather than of mathematics. Taking up the posi-
tion which Johannes Tinctoris established in *Diffinitorium
musices* (1474) that consonance and dissonance were to be
judged by ear only and not by numerical ratio, these
theorists established on the basis of subjective human
standards an equivalency between the *inventio* of rhetoric
and the *affectus exprimere* of musical form. Building
upon this equivalency, from Giovanni de' Bardi's *Discorso*

*mandato a Giulio Caccini* (1580) on, they increasingly allowed individual musical "figures" to correspond to rhetorical figures and musical composition to the rhetoric of the texts. "Even Monteverdi," Friedrich Blume notes in *Renaissance and Baroque Music,* "does not say that 'la parola' or 'la poesia' should be mistress of the music, but 'l'orazione.'"

Similarly, in poetry, as the predicaments of the lyric became selected more for their human expressiveness, the individual lover grew more pressing and anguished and his beloved more cruel and wooden, and, because of its increased responsibility, rhetoric was used more frequently than argument to resolve the situations. One need only compare Petrarch, who in his *Canzonieri* is pierced by the god of love at the sight of Laura, to Astrophel, who is moved not by Love, but directly by the beauty of Stella. In the first instance, Love is ultimately culpable for having pierced only Petrarch and not Laura, and all appeals must be made to him; in the second, Stella must be partially blamed for having flamed love's spark, and she becomes the more cruel for not having tended that flame. The effect throughout is similar to that distinction between Homeric gods and heroes which Rachel Bespaloff describes in *On the Iliad:* "Everything that happens has been caused by them [the gods], but they take no responsibility, whereas the epic heroes take total responsibility even for that which they have not caused." Their godliness comes precisely from their ability to walk away from situations which they have caused. In Petrarch, this disowning of responsibility by Love permits the speaker to reconcile himself to the loss of Laura. In Sidney, there are no outside irresponsible forces to acknowledge. The so-called "resignation" sonnets (numbers 109 and 110), which some editors have tacked on to "resolve" the sequence, are, as critics have indicated, not really part of the sequence. Their submission to higher forces is inconsistent with the entire drift of Astrophel's acceptance of responsibility.

The problem of the lyric at this time thus becomes one of how best to employ both the music and words of song so as to supply the needs of the would-be lover with a means to persuade his beloved that is approved by music and poetry theory and yet constitutes an effective image of reality. This task would require the artist and audience to agree to a mode of symbolism on which the lovers might rely and on which a rhetoric could be based. The symbolism would derive partly from the past, retaining, as had the medieval lyric, even in its most advanced reshaping, remnants of its previous form. The reshaping, moreover, would require public agreement involving revisions in music and poetry theory, the functions of the persona, and the structures of the lyric. As Gombrich suggests, it could be accomplished only by a long process of trial and error, in which both artist and audience took part.

In music, the preparations for such an agreement based upon symptomatic rather than mathematical symbols involved altering significative systems in at least five distinct areas. First, music theory had to allow the already mentioned blurring of musical and rhetorical figures into a single language. Second, it accepted a correspondence of word-content to emblematic tonal figures in a manner understood not from sensuous effect, but from abstract association. For example, the word "sun" (Latin, *sol*) would be set to the note G, the solmization syllable *sol*. It likewise accepted the closely related use of allegorical tonal figures for sensuous effects, descents by descending voices, ascents by ascending tones. It increased its use as well of *imitatio naturae,* or direct copying of sounds and noises such as chimes, bird songs, and storms. Lastly, it defined the expressive significance of the various keys. All these alterations shifted music away from its concerns as an *ars bene modulandi* to its new emphasis of obtaining its effects by means of a preconditioning of the audience.

In poetry, as the ultimate emphases of treatises like Sidney's *Apology* were given over to the poem's effect on its audience, its ability to move rather than instruct, the primary interest became rhetorical. Puttenham, for example, writing of love poetry, stated that it required a structure "variable, inconstant, affected, curious, and most witty of any others, whereof the joys were to be uttered in one sort, and sorrows in another, and, by the many forms . . . the many moods and pangs of lovers thoroughly to be discovered; the poor souls sometimes praying, beseeching, sometime honoring, advancing, praising, anotherwhile railing, reviling, and cursing, then sorrowing, weeping, lamenting; in the end, laughing, rejoicing, and solacing the beloved again, with a thousand delicate devices, odes, songs, elegies, ballads, sonnets, and other ditties." Already sharing with rhetoric a use of words, tropes, and colores, the lyric could without much difficulty accept the preconditioning which rhetoric had already given to the other branches of poetry. In so doing, it moved finally out of music into literary theory, where, as Jason de Nores' *Apologia* (1590) indicates, its place in an Aristotelian literary hierarchy is, by virtue of Aristotle's not having discussed it, made unsure. Here, Spingarn's view that the Renaissance had no systematic lyric theory makes its strongest appeal. Having left the systematic theory of music, the lyric finds itself in literary discussions given over to formal structures, style, and special conceits. Yet, the continuing high regard for it and the numerous references to its magical functions suggest that some of the old systematic framework obtains. The subject matter that Puttenham assigns to it, for instance, is particularly traditional. It divides into the medieval hierarchy of religious, political, and personal concerns. These attitudes suggest that there may not be any lessening of formality in the framework surrounding the lyric despite whatever new underpinnnings the interiorization may have given the whole.

Since, as in the matter of love conventions, the preparations for an agreed illusion of reality which were being made on the Continent were not exactly the same as those which were being made in England, some attention must be paid to both. In *The Praise of Music,* by reestablishing the relevance of music in Church services, John Case began as early as 1586 in England the drift away from Zwingli and back toward medieval and Italian music theory. Quoting Athanasius, he argues that to "sing Psalms artificially [in elaborate counterpoint] is not to make a show of cunning with our music . . . for . . . they that sing so, as the melody of words with the quantity of them, may well agree with the harmony of the spirit, be those which sing with the tongue and with understanding also. . . . For the soul being intentive to the words does forget the affections and perturbations: and being made merry with the pleasant sound is brought to a sense and feeling of Christ, and most excellent and heavenly cogitations." His arguments for the return of music to the Church and ultimately for accepting continental preparations were aided by the fact that the Zwinglian view of the non-transcendence of music and the actual banning of music from church services had not gained wholehearted support in England. Englishmen simply enjoyed singing too much and sought any occasion for it and any justification for its continuance. The major cathedrals had, moreover, through their reactionary composers, maintained a steady link with both the earlier English Catholic practices and Italy.

Added to these ties which had kept England's church music close to continental theory was a steady stream of Italian musicians imported for one reason or another into the English courts. Alfonso Ferrabosco, who was active at Elizabeth's court from 1562 to 1577, built up a rather exaggerated reputation there as a madrigalist despite an extremely conservative style of composition. As Kerman reconstructs the situation, "Interest in Italian music must have been constant, though taste did not remain the same. In the 1580's it was rather serious, adopting the European vogue for Marenzio; in the 1590's, under the influence of

Morley, it became lighter and more popular, reflecting superficially the new trends in Italian music." "Superficially," Kerman goes on to distinguish, "because it apprehended only the trite, insistent fashion for canzonet-like pieces, and ignored the amazing later devolpments of dramatic and pathetic expression." Some suggestion exists, also, to suppose that this interest shown by English composers in Italian music theory may have begun to accommodate previously formed literary interests.

But still, having once broken from Italy and from Rome, English composers did not go back completely to either. The madrigal did not become, as it had in Italy, "such a rage that even during Lent there was a great demand for spiritual madrigals in essentially the same style, set to sacred words." "The transposition of a decidedly secular style to sacred music, easy enough to the Latin mind," Kerman notes, "seemed less so to the English, particularly since the English secular madrigal itself was less serious, in general, than the Italian model. A solemn, unmadrigalesque native style was established in England for these 'exaltations.'" Other changes in musical taste had occurred to suggest that even had the English composers tried to go back completely to an Italian mode of writing, it would have been a slightly different mode from the one they left at mid-century. These changes in taste are due to the influence of the Netherlands composers, the work of the Florentine *camerata,* and the work of Jean de Baïf's *Académie de Poésie et de Musique.*

Kerman has pointed out the particular debt which English composers owe to the Netherlands in the matter of the madrigal. "At first one might suppose that Nicholas Yonge, the editor [of *Musica Transalpina* (1588)], had conceived the idea of issuing such a collection after having come in contact with some Italian anthologies of this sort. . . . But it appears that the English anthology is related not so much to Italian models as to Flemish ones, in particular to four very similar and well-received collections issued by Pierre Phalèse at Antwerp." Previously, while stressing the indebtedness of English madrigals to an English tradition, Fellowes also had noted an influence of the Flemish as well as the Italian: "It has already been said that the Flemings owed much to the English composers of Dunstable's time; thus in dealing with the influence of the foreign madrigalists of the sixteenth century upon our own school at the close of that century we are really tracing back to an influence which emanated originally from England." Lowinsky's work on *musica reservata* has indicated a more general debt to the Netherlands in the manner of composition as, in the hands of the Flemings, musical style shifted from a purely melodic-melismatic to a syllabic-declamatory character.

The English composer shares equally with his Italian counterpart the two remaining avenues of influence, perhaps without the advantage of an originally English basis on which to build. At their onsets, both the Florentine *camerata* and the French Academy expressed interest in the remarkable "effects" which were attributed by classical and biblical authorities to music. These effects of release and reintegration often constituted reconciliations resulting from mythic confrontations with forces outside the singer which defined his place, function, and character. Soon convinced by philosophical and historical authorities that neither poetry nor music singly could accomplish the effects described in classical and biblical accounts, commentators took their lead from Ficino, whom England even in Dean Colet's time had never completely accepted. In "De divino furore," Ficino identified the combination of music and poetry as the *furor poëticus,* the first of the intuitive, enthusiastic stages, in which the human soul, after its thorough discipline in all the separate arts, begins its interior ascent back to the original One. As Pontus de Tyard explained it for the French Academy, the soul, having reached in the body its lowest point of descent, is stunned and astonished. Meanwhile, the body is agitated and full of perturbations. From the combination of the two elements arises "a horrible discord and disorder." "Unless, by some means, this dreadful discord is transformed into a gentle symphony, and this impertinent disorder reduced to a measured equality, well and proportionately measured, and ordered in the gracious and grave facility of verses regulated by the careful observance of number and measure, the soul seems incapable of any just action." That is to say, as the tones allay and order the passion, the poetry at the same instant directs the reason, and, as a result, the soul is elevated a step further in its progress to perfection.

This now-interiorized reconciliation and elevation, based upon the necessarily exact union of music and words, is the avowed purpose of the Academy: "In order to bring back into use music in its perfection which is to represent words in singing completed by sounds, harmony and melody, consisting in the choice and regulation of voices, sounds, and well-harmonized accords, so as to produce the effect which the sense of the words requires, either lowering or raising or otherwise influencing the spirits, thus renewing the ancient fashion of composing measured verses to which are accommodated tunes likewise measured in accordance with metric art . . . we have agreed to form an Academy." A similar intention, in terms of basic principle, had been established in the *camerata,* where Vincenzo Galileo, the father of the famous scientist, attacked modern music (i.e., medieval polyphony) because, by obscuring the words with musical ornamentation and elaboration for the sake of the music itself, it neglected the highest part of music, which was the expression of the soul through words and music. Both academies, in the manner of Ficino, required an emphasis on words, and English composers, as Kerman states, "had little occasion, poetically speaking, to measure up to more serious expression, and consequently their styles are dominated by techniques developed by the Italians for their lighter forms of music." This minimization of the rational part (poetry) of the union of words and music by English composers corresponds to their minimization earlier in adopting foreign love conventions of objective (rational) proportion as the basis of attraction in love. In concert the minimizations may reflect a larger reluctance of the English character at this time to respond to the continental humanists' reduction of vast areas of human behavior to method.

The specific impact of the Florentine *camerata* and the French Academy is most apparent in the theory behind the Italian and English madrigal. In practice, however, only two English madrigalists, John Wilbye and John Ward, show the kind of literary taste so common among Italian composers in service of the academies. They are, moreover, among the most serious and best composers of the whole English school. The other composers tended to use lighter forms based upon texts of less literary interest and seldom competed by setting the same texts to different musical arrangements. Nevertheless, whether or not in practice these composers consciously responded favorably or unfavorably to the four basic principles of the academies, the principles affected their theory. Simplified, these principles maintained that only one note of music be set to one syllable; that homophonic rather than polyphonic settings be used; that notes be synchronized with the exact time and inflection of the words; and that coloration be employed to enhance understanding.

Since the poets do not influence either the acceptance of music theory or its practice directly, the precise role which they played in making the views of the academicians acceptable to English composers is difficult to determine. As James E. Phillips remarks in "Poetry and Music in the Seventeenth Century," although one cannot specifically describe the way in which the humanists' conception of the union of music and poetry reached England, the use by continental and English theorists of the same arguments and their citations from the same authorities leave no doubt that the ideal was shared. "One is tempted to speculate that the 'Areopagus' of Sidney and Spenser, which took over so many of the literary theories of the French academicians, also took over their views on the relationship of music and poetry." As neither Spenser nor Sidney writes directly of these relationships, perhaps nothing more should be ventured. Still, following Frances Yates, Phillips notes that "Sidney in the Apology describes poetry as suitable for music, observes that the ancient quantitative verse is more adaptable to music than modern accentual verse, and in his own experiments with quanti-tative verse in the *Arcadia* introduces each song with some indication of the instrument suitable to accompany it—all directly in line with de Baïf's injunctions about the classical relation of poetry and music." Likewise, although he leans more to medieval theory, Case cites the same authorities and employs the same arguments in his treatise as do the academicians to proclaim the supremacy of the union of music and words over either form independently.

Yet, however sincere their acceptance of the new symbolism of music and words and however fervent their propagation of it through their writings, these poets, perhaps because they were unable to accept completely the Petrarchan elements on which madrigal lyrics were based, tended to be most influential in areas other than the madrigal. It is clear that by the 1590's the composers had taken over completely the direction of the English madrigal. As Kerman notes most specifically of it in practice, "But though musical Italianization coincided in time with literary Italianization, it was not brought about by or even directly related to the literary movement. We may emphasize once again that the madrigal was never a literary form in England. It was not developed by poets, like the Italian madrigal, but imported piecemeal from abroad— imported, it seems clear, by musicians; nor did England adopt those elaborate and pedantic academies which in Italy maintained the art of music at the standards of the utmost literary purity. In comparison to the Italian, the English madrigal's purely musical bias is characteristic. . . . [It] had no real contacts with the serious poetry which fascinated the English literary circles, and which in a few years set up its own tradition and hallowed its own great masters."

Because of the basically literary nature of madrigal composition it may be best to establish the peculiar character of English madrigal verse, however slight its value, before embarking upon a discussion of madrigal music. Critics have generally agreed that the verse was relentlessly Petrarchan, pastoral, and Anacreontic in sentiment and style. Its suavity and mellifluousness aimed at expressing general moods rather than particular and personal experiences. Ranging from morbid, lachrymose, and melancholy to playful and lascivious, these moods stressed contrast to allow in turn contrasts in musical style. The sentiments the moods expressed were never without elaborate conceits and rarely without the most exaggerated protestations of lovers' heartaches. The stanzaic forms were varied. Preferably they were not strophic, since the Elizabethan conception of musical rhythm was never rigidly metrical. Frequent repetitions of phrases were advisable, short antithetical verbal expressions suitable, and refrains obviously appropriate. "The true madrigal," Fellowes goes on to note in *English Madrigal Verse 1588–1632*, "was seldom set to more than one stanza of poetry; and indeed these composers studied their words so closely and expressed themselves with such intimate regard for the particular meaning of each word and each phrase, that the exact repetition of their music to a fresh stanza of words was scarcely ever possible."

So far as the musical style of the madrigal is concerned, it was, first off, polyphonic. As Fellowes indicates, madrigal "took the form of unaccompanied song for at least three, and rarely for more than six, voice-parts. It was constructed mainly upon short musical phrases treated contrapuntally, with each voice-part having an equal share of the melodic interest, the musical phrases being taken up consecutively rather than simultaneously by the various voice-parts, the verbal phrases being several times re-iterated." He goes on to note that "every kind of device was employed by the composers both to secure variety and to sustain interest; and, above all considerations, they strove to add meaning and point to the words which they had chosen to set. It is especially in this last detail that they proved themselves supreme." He then distinguishes this kind of multiple part singing from the "ayre," adapted and harmonized for four voices. "This harmonized arrangement for combined voices not only closely resembled the harmonic part-song of later days, but may be regarded as its direct ancestor."

Of the various kinds of madrigals he classifies, Fellowes notes that "the canzonet and other such alternative terms, as used by the composers, do not imply any very material difference of constructive principles. The ballet is an exception; it is founded upon much more regular rhythmic outlines, having originally been an art-form in which singing and dancing were combined; and a distinctive feature of the ballet in the hands of the madrigalists was the introduction, at certain well-defined closes of words, of a passage of music sung to no regular words but to the syllables *fa la la.*" The printing of the music involved no bar lines of any kind for measurement, and the singer, unhampered by any obstacles like bars placed at regular intervals, was allowed to sing his music with the true ictus of the words, according to the aims of the academies and in exact accordance with the design of the composer. Fellowes concludes that "when the madrigal music is properly rendered, the *ictus* should fall exactly as it would do when the words are well spoken."

In *The English Madrigal Composers,* Fellowes points out that "madrigal-singing must have been in vogue in England for many years before the appearance in 1588 of Byrd's *Psalms, Sonnets, and Songs,* but it was of course mainly confined to the work of foreign composers as being practically the only music of the kind available. And this fashion was consistent with the Italian influence which showed itself so conspicuously in all branches of Art and Literature in England at that time." He then cites evidence that Italian madrigals, "sung in England with their original Italian words at least as early as 1564," had established a practical tradition prior to Thomas Morley's *Plain and Easy Introduction to Practical Music* (1597) for the would-be composer to follow. This tradition would allow the composer to learn his craft, as had the medieval song-writer, by choosing to follow either previous models or abstract theory or a combination of the two, while at the same time utilizing the matter his age had taught him to register. In this connection, Fellowes goes on to note that by the time the madrigal was imported, the work of English composers "followed the Italian design in its main features; but it bore a distinctive national stamp, and it even surpassed the work of the Italians in vitality and in the fertility and variety of imaginative expression, as well as in the boldness and originality of harmonic treatment. The very fact that the English madrigalists delayed their appearance until this late epoch was in itself a source of liberty which they were not slow to recognize; for by that time harmonic revolution was in the air, and the fetters which had bound fast the older generation of composers by the rigid rules of the modes were showing the first signs of giving way, albeit modal characteristics are abundantly evident throughout the music of these English composers."

In line with the rhetorical directions of madrigal music and lyrics, the persona of the lyric shed his anonymity. He became an advocate, choosing and conveying in song many of the positive values of his particular social class as he had learned by the device of predicaments to view these values. Although not so clearly delineated as Sidney's Astrophel, he, like Astrophel, was responsible for the emotive rather than the rational stress of the lyrics. As Morley described him, he was "possessed with an amorous humour." Turned signs or tokens, his words followed aesthetic rather than cognitive frames and aimed toward defining human limits rather than suggesting superhuman realms. Moreover, as in sustained autobiography, neither he nor the personality a listener abstracted from the song was ever quite the actual lyricist. Nevertheless, as with every work of art, a listener's tendency to abstract from the madrigal a picture of its creator based upon this persona would be met not only by what the words displayed but also by qualities which the lyricist may not have deliberately employed. In both circumstances, the utilitarian function of books given by the humanists to teach methodology in the arts would have moved art away from a tradition of pure imitation.

On the specific matter of the four points which the academies had laid down for the reformation of music, in its development of a "distinct national stamp," English madrigal practice tended to disregard the principle of homophonic music altogether and was not strictly faithful to the other three points. For example, control of the length and rhythmic values of notes to suit words is less common in English than in continental music, and coloration had less effect on its form. In English madrigals, coloration rarely created the form as it did in Italian music. Rather it was contained within the form. This was also true of the motet, which Morley indicates in theory might be more susceptible to the work of the academies. Because of its divine subject matter, it was deemed by him the highest form of composition and the most protective of language. He declares that "this kind of all others which are made on a ditty, requires most art, and moves and causes most strange effects in the hearer, . . . for it will draw the auditor (and specially the skilful auditor) into a devout and reverent kind of consideration of Him for whose praise it was made." Yet, the motet's construction, like the madrigal's, proved rigidly formal, always polyphonic, and more protective of form than tolerant of excessive coloration.

Insofar as the English composers did come under the sway of the French Academy and the Florentine *camerata,* it was in the revival and development of the lutenist ayre. Here, while preserving the elements of structure, they made their pleas for homophony, simplicity, and naturalness of diction. Utilizing a solo voice with a chordal instrumental accompaniment, the form allowed the meaning of the words and their human significance to be immediately comprehensible. As Fellowes describes the characteristics of the form in *English Madrigal Verse 1588–1632,* "The ayres of the lutenists usually took the form of solo-songs with several stanzas of words, for each of which, as a general rule, the same music was repeated. . . . When performed as solo-songs they were accompanied with the lute, reinforced by a base viol or some such instrument, to add support and body to the general effect." In *Elizabethan Music and Musical Criticism,* M. C. Boyd indicates that the form was a uniquely native development without parallel on the Continent and dating from the Elizabethan time. Kerman adds that the praise which "has been so generously showered upon [the Elizabethan song] since has been intended mainly for the lyrics of the lute-air, which in reprints and anthologies of the last hundred years have customarily been printed together with real madrigal verse (often without any distinction drawn between the kinds of music concerned). These lute-air sets certainly contain very valuable poetry, and are indeed sometimes more interesting as literature than as music." "In the solo ayre with lute," Mellers writes, "we find the most advanced experiments towards a theatrical style."

Whereas the musical structure of a madrigal took its lead from its words, the reverse was true of the ayre. Its structure, like that of the Tudor song, often influenced the form of the words to which the music would eventually be joined. This music was constructed upon a first stanza, whereupon subsequent stanzas might be written to accord with its close union. Thus, for example, in Thomas Campion's "Author of Light" as in Wyatt's lyrics, one has several stanzas (in this case, two) written to the same melodic pattern. *Expolitio* keeps their movements emotionally exact, the emotions of the first stanza returning in the course of the second. However, here, due to the musical coloration, far more rigid emotional correspondences than those practiced by Wyatt have to be maintained:

Author of light, revive my dying sprite;
Redeem it from the snares of all-confounding night.
Lord, light me to thy blessèd way,
For blind for blind with worldly vain desires I wander as
    astray.
Sun and moon, stars and underlights I see,
But all their glorious beams are mists and darkness being
    compared to thee.

Fountain of health, my soul's deep wounds recure:
Sweet show'rs of pity rain, wash my uncleanness pure.
One drop of thy desirèd grace
The faint the faint and fading heart can raise and in joy's
    bosom place.
Sin and death, hell and tempting fiends may range,
But god his own will guard, and their sharp pains and grief
    in time assuage.

As Mellers notes in his discussion of the score, for the
noble fifth which accompanies "Author of light" in the
first stanza, there is a corresponding "Fountain of health"
in the second. For the syncopation, melisma, and dis-
onance of "deep wounds," there is "dying sprite." "Sweet
show'rs of pity" replace the redemption of the opening
stanza, and "uncleanness," the "confounding night." The
faint and fading heart and the blind wanderings of lines
four of each stanza serve the same musical purpose. "Sin
and death, hell and tempting fiends," though convenient
dualisms, are not allegorically appropriate to the phrase
built upon the falling fifth by "Sun and moon, stars and
underlights." On the other hand, the assuagement of
"sharp pains and grief" is perfect for the chromatic ascent
established in "mists and darkness being." Moreover, there
is in the manner of exact union of words and music
nothing in the words which encourages the auditor to
linger. The poetry appears deliberately designed to allow
for the anticipatory drive of music.

Although better in quality than the pre-Petrarchan
lyric, the ayre lyric, by virtue of its having to evoke several
corresponding predicaments that enlist identical emo-
tional responses, remains generalized. However much its

critics have insisted that its coldness and impersonality can be offset by musical accompaniment, the lyric still does not possess a clear-cut persona, nor does it become a fully-fleshed expression of consciousness. In ayres like Campion's, *contentio* seems to be relegated almost mechanically to complete lines rather than to phrases within each line. Perhaps of necessity, in order to introduce the listener immediately to the joy-despair-joy movement of the piece, he uses "light" and "health" to contrast with "dying" and "wounds" in the opening lines of each stanza. Nevertheless, typical of composers in the form generally, he has used no transitions between stanzas which might have allowed either a narrative, logical, or an emotive progression to evolve. The stanzas present two distinct (but emotionally congruent and hence emotionally repetitive) moods, set to identical musical phrases.

One has only to compare the achievement of this kind of lyric, based on the ayre, to the carefully modulated classical balance of the lyric whichWilbye set to a madrigal score to see the difference in direction that words for music commonly took when the continental frame of the academies was essayed:

> O wretched man, why lov'st thou earthly life,
> Which nought enjoys but cares and endless trouble?
> What pleasure here but breeds a world of grief?
> What hour's ease that anguish does not double?
> No earthly joys but have their discontents;
> Then loathe that life which causeth such laments.

In this lyric, all lines but the last build upon Petrarchan paradoxes, which would enlist comparable musical rises and falls. The frequency of these paradoxes forces rapid changes of mood. Since the poem chooses to address its audience, these changes of mood are designed to move the listener and to aid him in his self-discovery. To judge from the fierceness of his *contemptus mundi* and his tantalizing evocation of its pleasures, the speaker of the poem is obviously a preacher, and one can envision a listener squirming in his own new religious self-awarenesses. Yet the brevity of the form prevents the development of a persona as fully various as Astrophel and reveals merely a single state of mind.

Aesthetically what the rapidity of the poem's changes in mood should accomplish is to turn the flow of the song back upon itself as its own subject. In the excessiveness of these changes and movements, the equilibrium of psychic continuity and the *virtu* of genteel reserve and self-control, which were parts of the Tudor lyric, transform into a drive of the *affecto* for fulfillment and display. The result would be similar to that effect of baroque art, whose purpose, as E. I. Watkin indicates in *Catholic Art and Culture,* is to "infuse strict boundaries and well-defined shapes [here set by the reversals of mood] with a sense of the Infinite beyond, yet within." In *The Style of Palestrina and the Dissonance,* Knud Jeppesen remarks how this infusion of boundaries should work in music, not as a release, but as a definition of the persona: "The older music, 'Musica mondana,' has a quality that seems to open out upon the universe, something cosmic. It is as though this music frees itself of individualistic bonds, glides away and dissolves into space. Of the newer music, 'Musica humana,' it might be figuratively said that it also strikes against the limits of the individual, but is hurled back upon itself and condensed into the individually characteristic. The tension arising from this process of condensation finds its resolution in the accent (in its extreme form, the free dissonance). The two [epochs] separate at this point, for only the new music has the violent, vehement emphasis."

Blume agrees that the result of these changes of mood is "an inflamed self-consciousness, an ego-cult that verges on narcissism, a boundless urge to abandon the soul to all torments and delights, from a suicidally contrite, agonizing consciousness of sin to ecstatic release in the celestial radiance of divine mercy," but he cautions against attributing to English music at this time any of these full-blown tendencies of Baroque. Because the English composer rarely allowed "word-painting" to create (dictate) the form of this music, it is difficult to regard his work as Baroque. John Dowland, who was personally involved in the religious battles of the Counter Reformation, may be an exception. He takes on a characteristically baroque attitude and, around 1600, with his songs and instrumental works, inaugurates a pronounced English baroque. Nevertheless, by making his work partly the imitation of external models (actions, events, noises, etc.) and partly the expression of inner agitation (psychic states, emotions), the English composer was obviously moving much earlier than 1600 toward the full-blown Baroque.

Moreover, since madrigal verse at this time inclined to make verse-technique its theme as well as its operative mode, its effect resembled that described by Roland Barthes in *Writing Degree Zero* as characteristic of French writing since 1850. Literature had become "an object, through promoting literary labour to the status of value; form became the end product of craftsmanship, like a piece of pottery or a jewel." Here one need only recall Ronsard's remark about grand style's making "verse glitter like precious stones on the fingers of some great lord" to be made aware of the Petrarchist's similar aim. In the promotion of this craft as labor, emotions, now diverted from a primarily denotative stress, shine forth above the sequence of their relationships; and grammar, bereft of its function, becomes merely the device for the presenting and spacing of these emotions. With the abolishment of these linear connections of grammar, emotions are left only with their vertical, Faustian projections. They loom like monoliths or pillars which plunge one into a totality of meanings, reflexes, and recollections. The effect of these techniques as they condense becomes finally a stasis of self-indulgence, which, in their refusal to adopt fully, the English composers failed to develop as an avenue for full self-expressiveness.

At the same time, by establishing alterations in the significative systems of music whereby it might become more expressive of human emotions without using words, the evolving process of this agreed illusion of reality prepared for the triumph of instrumental music. The re-valuation began modestly enough. As Reese indicates, the instrumental settings of the dance exerted "a particularly strong influence on English chamber music from about

1500 to shortly before 1560." To this influence was added the influence of the more ambitious, but vocal *In nomine* and *miserere* settings of later composers and finally that of the nonvocal fantasias of Byrd, Morley, and others. One might suspect that the revaluation, if it had philosophical justification in other than popular appeal, occurred because these instrumental pieces were essentially words-for-music pieces without the words. In them, the motions of the mind (in memory) would have been brought to bear upon the passions of the body (music) in a manner consistent with Augustine's differentiation between phantasia and phantasm. The first was a memory of things experienced; the second, an extension of memory to things never experienced. In this way, instrumental music could assume its place above words and music without any new treatises.

In *The English Madrigal Composers*, Fellowes assigns the triumph of instrumental over vocal music to the commonly accepted date—the year 1600. He comments on the effect in England: "Just so long as instrumental composition occupied a subordinate position in the scheme of musical development, English musicians were found in the foremost place, but so soon as the relative position of vocal and instrumental music became reversed, the music of this country ceased at that same moment to occupy a position of the first importance." Campion's objection in *A Book of Ayres* (1601) to the excessive coloration involved in the imitative character of madrigal music offers an unexpected and telling clue to why English musicians fell in stature as well as a possible explanation of why England never developed musically the full ranges of self needed for opera: "The nature of every word is precisely expressed in the note, like the old exploded action in comedies, when if they did pronounce Memeni, they would point to the hinder part of their heads, if Video, put their finger in their eye. But such childish observing of words is altogether ridiculous, and we ought to maintain as well in notes, as in action a manly carriage, gracing no word, but that which is eminent and emphatical." This "manly carriage"—itself a mark of social awareness that removes man from the unfallen state of a "natural" union of words and music—is a mask; it is worn by a man without sufficient self-awareness to permit him to recombine words and music through self-conscious stylization. It is the response to contemporary life, which in *Music and Society* Mellers states occupied the Elizabethan poets so fully that they had no time to work with professional musicians on a new alliance.

In the function and development of the persona, the extent to which this mask was used and its relationship to contemporary life are clearly revealed. As a device for defining an acceptable agreed illusion of reality, the persona evolved along lines of expression different from those expressive devices utilized by music. Although its conception was already long anticipated by Dante's statement in the *Convivio* (*c.* 1300) that the "I" of his poetry was not himself, the "I" of most English poetry had identified itself not with the poet as a physical and social entity but with the poet as singer. Yet, as Wright points out, the dimensions of the poet's personality even at this rudimentary stage became subtly various. In a sense, all that was in the poem revealed what he was; in another sense, each particular character, momentary attitude, habit of reflection, and turn of phrase was drawn from what he had learned of himself as Alpert's "real" individual as well as from much both within and outside of him that he had never consciously observed. His poems named objects, people, events, and sought to give meaning through their conceits and arrangements of material.

Now that music and words were supposed to present an event in such a way that the listener saw it before his very eyes, the poet's ability to give meaning became contingent upon his ability to probe the inner resources of imagination and memory which, since before the time of Cicero, had been part of rhetoric. This probe required the poet's subscription to some of the mnemonic notions popular at the time that certain tokens evoke situations in the minds of people, and to the belief that finally, as Augustine posited in Book X of his *Confessions,* God (truth) was also inward dwelling, innate in memory. Therefore, for music to engage in a rhetoric of exuberance and self-indulgence, the poet must first select proper tokens, including the lyric's persona, and do so along lines that would make the persona an effective instrument of memory. The idea that by naming objects one acquires mastery over them and by fixing them in song one asserts their meaning thus takes on new meaning. Song does not convey the meaning of objects or give mastery over them, but as a speaking picture (*ut pictura poesis*) verifies their truth. The vividness by which the reader is moved to reconstruct mentally the place of these objects becomes a test of the poem's *energia*. As Shakespeare describes the process in his sonnets 14 and 16, truth (inward worth) and beauty (outward fair) must thrive together. This joint life is the source of the immortality which the Elizabethan poet promises to bestow upon his subjects and whose success requires his attention not only to the persona but also to both heart and ornament. In accordance with Sidney's example of "writing *Canidia* upon a most sweet face," the illusion of reality exists as the persona arouses both an objective world and an inner truth into a special visual significance only available through his presence and not through any exact copying. As such, the conceit of poetic immortality, whose history John traces through Pindar, Sappho, Cicero, Horace, Vergil, Propertius, Ovid, and Ronsard, undergoes a subtle and important alteration.

In addition to this mnemonic function of the lyric persona, there are other functions which prove relevant. In perceiving that his attitudes "are stylized according to contemporary conventions" and change with the changes in these conventions, Wright provides insight into the sociological values implicit in the persona which prevent the lyric from assuming its own complete sense of order, justice, and probability, and thereby the conscious stylizations of self that might permit its remerging with music into opera. Wright notes, for example, that "the qualities and social status of lyric personae . . . change in England as the political and economic center of gravity shifts from the aristocracy to the middle class . . . and continues its downward path through the seventeenth and eighteenth centuries. In weakened form the courtly poetry persists, and its courtly persona still meets the expectations of a courtly reader, still claims no superiority over him. But the 'I' employed by the metaphysical poets is clearly lower in social standing than that of Wyatt or Surrey or Spenser or Shakespeare, not because the poet is of lower rank, but because the audience is." In England, because of the tensions of the Tudor monarchies which led to the creations of new consorts of nobility out of middle class merchants and statesmen, and because of the emphasis which the Protestants put on literacy as a means to man's salvation, this popular audience came into existence perhaps earlier than in either France or Italy.

These differences extend even into the subject matter of the poems. The lovers of Sidney and Spenser are based ostensibly on models approved by aristocratic tastes, whereas, by displaying intellection and sincerity rather than social grace and decency, the lovers of later poets like Donne and Shakespeare demonstrate their middle-class biases. In *Renaissance Literary Criticism,* Vernon Hall explains the discrepancy by observing that as the poet should be of noble birth and publication was considered beneath the dignity of an aristocrat, so long as artistocrats wrote, an air of *sprezzatura* or "sweet disorder" was deliberately cultivated to give an impression of graceful negligence and seemingly effortless production, and this impression carried into the formation of the persona. In contrast, the professional writer tended to make his productions more relevant through urgency. This negligence on the part of the artistocrat is deceptive: as Sidney gives witness in his discussion of the art of memory in his *Apology*, it is belied by its own intense seriousness.

Providing still clearer insight into the nature of the persona is the contrast between the Renaissance attitude of a union of subject and object by memory devices and the post-Enlightenment belief in more complete fusions brought about by a total interiorization. The contrast is particularly interesting in its illustration of how changes in thought-pattern do alter personae. "In Renaissance lyrics," Wright notes, "the persona as singer typically comments on human experience, sings it, names it, treats it in the special manner of poems. In the typical Romantic lyric, the persona goes through an experience, recounting it as he proceeds." The function of the persona in the sixteenth-century lyric thus becomes similar to that of the transpersonal agent binding Ficino's lovers. He localizes the action, gives life-sense to the poem, and offers an object with whom the listener can sympathize. Like Ficino's agent, he binds not within himself but within his presence the inward worth and outward fair that must together thrive. Depending upon the direction of his persuasion, he presents these unions in a good light or a bad one, since he forms the locus by which the acceptability of the tokens, and hence their senses of reality, is accomplished not by a principle of causality, but by a principle of contiguity. The persona of the Renaissance poem need not undergo personally the experience of the outside world in order to fuse it to an inner truth. He need only be contiguous to it. The Romantic notion that by experiencing the outer world it may be interiorized through memory, fused, and returned, reinterpreted by its effects, is quite different.

As a narrowness brought about by restricting the range of musical coloration made the stylization of Elizabethan music unacceptable for the vaster consciousness of self that was being felt in the poetry, precisely the ability of the sonnet sequence to act as an adequate vehicle for self-consciousness made such sequences popular. Groups of sonnets could extend one's knowledge of self because they could, after Sidney, develop more closely and more fully the ranges of personality and action which self-consciousness demanded for a life-sense. But there were other reasons as well. The uses which Wyatt and Sidney make of Petrarch to define their own un-Petrarchan notions lets one recognize the wisdom of Wright's warning: "As everything within the poem comes more and more to be a reproduction of actual things and people outside it, and the 'I' becomes increasingly the poet himself, the poem runs the risk of losing the peculiar properties of poems." It was in part to preserve these properties of poems while at the same time establishing through Petrarch a mirror of a false world against which to esteem and know the real one that the sonnet sequence became especially significant.

In such circumstances, for the Elizabethan court—as had been the case earlier—the basis for selecting such mirrors was the acceptability of their world views. Love poetry specifically, since in it the audience and lover were one, quite often had to be handled so that, were the audience enlarged, the illusion of reality on which the poem was based would still be viable regardless of whether or not the love was identified. Thus, like Canidia, whose "sweet portrait" bears only mnemonic connection with her, "who, Horace swears, was foul and ill-favored," the woman of the sequence would often have only "writing" to identify her. Penelope Rich, who may be the Stella of Sidney's *Astrophel and Stella,* provides an excellent analogue: She is nothing like her poetic portrait. Petrarch and the Petrarchists and their sonnet sequences which set the standards of social behavior in love throughout the courts of Europe forced those poets who wished to appear courtly and in love to choose the sonnet sequence, the Petrarchan mode, and Petrarchan tokens for their expression, and for remodeling their Canidias accordingly.

Since, like Sidney, the early English Petrarchans had not completely accepted Petrarch, and, in the case of the later Petrarchists, many did so for the mnemonic as well as the romantic qualities that obtained in the *Canzonieri,* their use of Petrarchan models resulted in various kinds of sonnet sequences. Of these, the most baffling to a modern reader is the mnemonics sequence. This sequence, which relies upon the notion developed in the Renaissance that Petrarch was a master of artificial memory, utilizes devices (*loci*) to commit things to memory where they may be recalled by place rather than by fable. Citing in his *Apology* the reasons why verse exceeds prose in knitting up the memory, Sidney gives evidence of such practice: "Lastly, even they that have taught the Art of memory have showed nothing so apt for it as a certain room divided into many places well and thoroughly known.

Now, that has the verse in effect perfectly, every word having its natural seat, which seat must needs make the words remembered." This room (stanza) would locate the items (tokens), mentally placed within it, and let the mind, in merging inner and outer reality, retrace the sequence of these items. The use of these rooms is similar to the golden chain in oratory which Sidney cites in sonnet 58 of *Astrophel and Stella*. The sources of these *loci* or rooms could be real life, the imagination, or, in some cases, numerical sequences. Spenser, who had, as both A. Kent Hieatt in *Short Time's Endless Monument* and Alastair Fowler in *Spenser and the Numbers of Time* indicate, a propensity for developing the substructures of his work mathematically (magically), seems likewise to have begun his *Amoretti* sequence with a mathematical substructure. The work opens with a poem whose imagery descends along a sequence of threes from page to line to rhyme while at the same time ascending from vegetable to animal to rational. The same chiasmic structure continues in the next three sonnets which move from the interior ("unquiet thought") to the exterior (nature) and at the same time record births—singly, dually, and plurally. The purpose of these progressions is not to tell a story, but to evoke a series of responses that will magically prove self-revelatory.

Nevertheless, since one's sense of personality comes not from a sequence of tokens, but from a sequence of causal responses to action, the mnemonic sonnet sequence is less popular than the other two sequences which critics identify. The first of these is, as Jean Robertson insists in

142

"Sir Philip Sidney and His Poetry," the narrative sequence: "Those who close their eyes to the fact that a story is being told and who persist in treating the sonnets as meditations on love or explorations of the lover's emotions not only ignore the nature of the sonnet cycle but also disregard the purpose of the Renaissance lyric—to persuade and to praise. The primary purpose of a sonnet was to 'get favour.' Sidney is, of course, only half-serious when he criticizes lyrics for failing in this respect." Her statements are in reply to C. S. Lewis' contention in *English Literature in the Sixteenth Century* that "the first thing to grasp about the sonnet sequence is that it is not a way of telling a story. It is a form which exists for the sake of prolonged lyrical meditation, chiefly on love, but relieved from time to time by excursions into public affairs, literary criticism, compliment, or what you will. External events—a quarrel, a parting, an illness, a stolen kiss—are every now and then mentioned to provide themes for meditation." " 'Look in thy heart and write,' " he adds, "is good counsel for poets; but when a poet looks in his heart he finds many things there besides the actual. That is why, and how, he is a poet."

But Samuel Taylor Coleridge seems to have understood what neither Robertson nor Lewis, who take extreme positions, will recognize: the narrative line of the sequence is well known to the audience and to the girl. It has been accepted by both as an operative rather than a thematic scheme in self-consciousness as tokens had been accepted as operative in memory practices. One need only mention that the sonnet sequences of three very respected poets—

Petrarch, Spenser, and Shakespeare—make little sense taken either as straight narratives or as straight lyrical meditations. Although the order of the Shakespeare sequence is rightly in question, there is no doubt that both Petrarch and Spenser set the order of their works. Moreover, were the "problem" of Shakespeare's *Sonnets* merely one of arrangement, he might have issued an authorized edition to correct this error as he did with many of his plays which were pirated in bad copies. It is clear that the blocks and abrupt shifts in the sequences must be intended to work in another way, perhaps like the strict boundaries of Baroque music, hurling the reader back upon himself so as to compress his emotions into a vertical self-indulgence whose end is self-definition. Within this self-indulgence and the general practice of using Petrarch's long love-pursuit and anguish as a mirror against which to gauge and know his own feelings, the poet would be able to condense, alter, or redo expanses of the *Canzonieri* into the course of fourteen lines, or, in a sequence of sonnets, arrange the narrative sense of his romance along what Ford Madox Ford would later call "the time shift device." Basically he would be arranging his poems so that image and idea were interwoven as Ovid had interwoven them in his *Metamorphoses,* in a manner reminiscent of the weavings of recurrent themes in musical composition. The structure of the sonnet sequence would approximate no fixed pattern, but, as Coleridge notes in chapter xvi of his *Biographia Literaria,* it would rely mainly upon a harmony of the whole, achieved like stochastic music by a combination of unpremeditated narrative and lyrical flights:

144

The imagery is almost always general: sun, moon, flowers, breezes, murmuring streams, warbling songsters. . . . The fable of their narrative poems, for the most part drawn from mythology, or sources of equal notoriety, derive their chief attractions from the manner of treating them; from impassioned flow, or picturesque arrangement. . . . The excellence at which they aimed, consisted in the exquisite polish of the diction, combined with perfect simplicity . . . by the studied position of words and phrases, so that not only each part should be melodious in itself, but contribute to the harmony of the whole, each note referring and conducing to the melody of all the foregoing and following words of the same period or stanza; and lastly with equal labour, the greater because unbetrayed, by the variation and various harmonies of their metrical movement . . . by countless modifications and subtle balances of sound in the common metres of their country.

Thus, centuries before James Joyce and T. S. Eliot defined the "epical" or "mythic" approach to literature for the modern reader, the Renaissance had developed it. Based not on psychology but probably upon a typology derived from the early Church Fathers and from classical writers and modified by the Renaissance writers' new abilities to view themselves "in perspective," this mythic consciousness made itself part of the age's self-consciousness. Like Ficinian "consciousness," it required the mind to divide itself into two—past and present—and to confront itself with the vehicle of a patterned past as the metaphoric tenor for its present mood and then by more knowledge to overcome the separation. In the *Canzonieri,* it had permitted Petrarch to hinge his pursuit of Laura on Ovid's account of Apollo's unsuccessful pursuit of Laurel, punning as he proceeded on Laura's name, "lauro" (laurel), "l'aura" (breeze), and "l'auro" (gold). As a result, rather than acquiring the qualities of a successful action, the pursuit took on from its inception both the general qualities of metaphor, and, for modern readers, the more specific qualities of the Absurd quest of Albert Camus' Sisyphus. It committed one to the struggle rather than to the resolution of the struggle, and allowed Petrarch to indulge both himself and his reader in its leisurely prog- ress and reversals. Within this consciousness—as within the Ovidian legend—life turned into art. Life could so metamorphose because the element of contingency in mythic living is absent; one has only art's false world of metaphor, with its reliances upon causality and predeter- mination. In such predetermination, Spenser's persona in sonnet 18 of the *Amoretti* sequence can be rebuffed by a girl who decides she has had enough of prescribed be- havior:

> But when I plead, she bids me play my part,
>    and when I weep, she says tears are but water:
>    and when I sigh, she says I know the art,
>    and when I wail she turns herself to laughter.

Later, in *A Portrait of the Artist as a Young Man,* when Joyce pictures this "mythic" approach as having emerged out of the lyrical form, he distinguishes it from the lyric form by the artist's prolonged brooding "upon himself as the centre of an epical event . . . till the centre of emo- tional gravity is equidistant from the artist himself and from others." He assigns the form two complications that the lyric form lacks. In addition to emotion, the artist must have an epical event—in this case, the model of the Petrarch love sequence—and, to express his emotions, the poet must develop a persona or voice which is as well drawn and objective as any of the other personages of his poem. In Joyce, this persona would be derived from a specific work of art which life imitates. In the Renaissance lyric, the persona was usually the poet objectified by his acceptance of a clearly defined role as poet-lover, the man as he knew himself to be by measurement against the Petrarchan model. For nonlyric poetry, the Renaissance poet chose different masters so that he never integrated his life-style into a harmony based on one model. In his bringing together after the manner of Castiglione these contradictory impulses and disparate, fragmented experiences, he preserved his free will and originality by the very uniqueness which style required him to impose on relationships, rhythms, accents, and symmetries. As T. S. Eliot rightly explained of the "epical" persona in "Ulysses, Order, and Myth," "It is simply a way of controlling, of ordering, of giving a shape and a significance to the immense panorama of futility and anarchy which is contemporary history." The transition of the Elizabethan world view from Catholicism to Protestantism, from Ptolemy to Copernicus, from aristocratic to middle-class power, from European to global perspectives, must have seemed to its citizens no less filled with the sense of futility and anarchy than the world view which imposed itself after World War I on the writers of the twenties.

# CHAPTER FIVE

# John Donne

❧ The predicaments that sowed the seeds for the shift of the lyric into the narrative and epic genres also sowed the seeds for its possible shift into the dramatic form. As Joyce has indicated, this form would be reached when the vitality with which the poet has saturated his personages "fills every person with such vital force that he or she assumes a proper and intangible esthetic life." Infused with this vital force, the characters of a work would take on an identity independent of the poet's persona and become an expression of this identity independent of the poet. The saturation, as described by Cassirer in *Language and Myth* in regard to the mythic imagination, inexplicably involves some transference of energy: "When, on the one hand, the entire self is given up to a single impression, is 'possessed' by it [the impression] and, on the other hand, there is the utmost tension between the subject and its object, the other world; when external reality is not merely viewed and contemplated, but overcomes a man in sheer immediacy, with emotions of fear or hope, terror or wish fulfillment: then the spark jumps somehow across, the tension finds release, as the subjective excitement becomes objectified, and confronts the mind as a god or a daemon." In the case of Donne, whose early interests are social rather than mythic, what is objectified is that world of contemporary life to which, as Mellers points out, poetic drama appealed and from which English composers excluded themselves by their refusals to develop fully self-expressive forms.

This shift to dramatic interests increasingly let predicaments take on a function similar to that described in Aristotle's *Rhetoric* and endorsed later by the advocates of *musica reservata*. Poems sought to present scenes before the eye of the listener and thereby engage his feelings. In fact, scenes in Donne's poetry are so completely realized before the poet begins his opening line that Donne often feels he does not have to spend time in the poem on mere description. Thus, the force of the clear mental picture (*energia*) makes possible an avoidance of the visual for what Donne critics have called a transformation into states of mind and feeling. This transformation approximates what Aristotle calls the activation of metaphors for the purpose of liveliness. Its incorporation into poetry occurs just about the time when, as Panofsky indicates in *Idea*, the "idea" was no longer present a priori in the mind of the artist, but was brought forth by him a posteriori: "From now on an idea no longer 'dwells' or 'pre-exists' in the soul of the artist, as Cicero and Thomas Aquinas had put it, and still less is it 'innate' to him, as genuine

Neoplatonism had expressed it. Rather 'it comes into his mind,' 'arises,' is 'derived' from reality, 'acquired,' nay, 'formed and sculpted.' " This reconception of idea made the flow of ideas individual and, as such, the subject for self-analysis, though not in the same way that Immanuel Kant would allow the mind in analysis to create its own reality. As one anonymous nineteenth-century critic expressed it for the *Retrospective Review* (1823): "Accordingly, however intense a feeling might be, or however noble a thought, it was to be heightened and illustrated, in the expression of it, by clustering about it a host of images and associations (congruous or not, as it might happen), which memory or imagination, assisted by the most quick-eyed wit, or the most subtle ingenuity, could in any way contrive to link it." In short, the singularity of the associations which Donne's "quick-eyed wit" clustered about his feelings and thoughts would in their characterizations of mutable predicaments reveal much to him about his own nature.

Characterizing the elements of the transformation which give to Donne's poetry its sense of inwardness or thought, Theodore Redpath relates in his Introduction to *The Songs and Sonnets* that "the focus of attention is rarely the visual aspect of experience. The rarity of auditory sensations is even more marked. . . . There is, indeed, scarcely any reference to sounds at all. Again, sense-impressions of smell as distinct from taste do not seem to occur. . . . There are, on the other hand, a few references to sensations of taste, and a fair number to the motor sensations involved in sucking, feeding, drinking, and swallowing

. . . also . . . organic sensations, such as the sense of inflammation of the veins which love may cause, or the sensation of 'sorrowing dulness' after sexuality." Redpath concludes that "in point of fact, in the *Songs and Sonnets* motor and organic sensations definitely predominate over sensations of sight, sound, smell, taste, and even touch, and that is so even if we include in 'touch' cutaneous sensations of temperature as well as pressure. This probably accounts for a feeling of *inwardness* that one quite frequently senses in the poems, despite all their references to the outside world."

In his *Rhetoric,* Aristotle accounts for the special ability of the technique to create scenes while at the same time avoiding description and being inward. He sees it as a matter of language which has been charged properly with emotion:

For emotion, if the subject be wanton outrage, your language will be that of anger; if you speak of impiety or filth, use the language of aversion and reluctance even to discuss them; if of praiseworthy deeds, the language of admiration; if of piteous things, that of dejection; and similarly for the other emotional states. The appropriateness of your language to the emotion will make people believe in your facts. In their souls they infer, illegitimately, that you are telling the truth, because they, in a like situation, would be moved in the same way as you are; accordingly, even when the facts are not as the speaker says, the audience think he is right. Indeed, they are always in sympathy with an emotional speaker even when there is nothing in what he says; and that is why many an orator tries to stun the audience with sound and fury.

Likewise, Richmond has pointed out that "energetic poets from the earliest times have known how to jar the reader into attention by such effects as the opening of Rufinus' epigram: 'Don't embrace a skinny woman . . .' or Nicharchus' equally brusque admonition opening another *Greek Anthology* epigram: 'Don't listen to your mother, Philumena.' " Thus, by having realized his scenes before he began his poems, Donne is capable of involving the audience by letting them immediately overhear a monologue spoken to an inamorata, or to the god of love, or occasionally to a third person. Sometimes, as in "Song: Go and catch a falling star," the reader is directly engaged. At other times, as in "The Canonization," there is a brusque, disarming beginning: "For God's sake, hold your tongue, and let me love." Always, as Aristotle has suggested, the appropriateness of the language to its emotions makes people believe in the poem's "facts."

Donne's particular skill in this area of charging his language emotionally so as to influence his audence's belief has long enlisted the praise of critics. In his *Rhetoric* (1828), Thomas De Quincey called Donne "the first very eminent rhetorician in the English literature," laying emphasis in doing so upon the "original use of the word . . . as laying the principal stress upon the management of the thoughts, and only a secondary one upon the ornaments of style." Similarly, in his Introduction to *Metaphysical Lyrics & Poems of the Seventeenth Century*, Sir Herbert Grierson praises Donne's management of thoughts, illustrating how it stylistically "secures two effects, the troubling of the regular fall of the verse stresses by the intrusion of rhetorical stress on syllables which the metrical pattern leaves unstressed, and, secondly, an echoing and re-echoing of similar sounds parallel to his fondness for resemblances in thoughts and things apparently the most remote from one another." Earlier, in *The Rhetoric of John Donne's Verse,* Wightman Fletcher Melton had noted some of this combination of rhetoric and ornament when he was tracing Donne's use of the same words and sounds in arsis and thesis. He concluded that "while the verses of other poets rime in the middle or at the end, Donne's rime everywhere."

A valuable comparison between Donne's charging of language emotionally for the rhetorical management of thoughts and sounds and their management by musical structure is furnished by Arnold Stein in *John Donne's Lyrics*. In deciding to deal with the ornamental rather than the rhetorical stress of Donne's technique, he designates the previously noted echoing and re-echoing of sounds, "the musical effects" of the poetry. Writing of "The Good-morrow," he asserts, "The poem *is* a musical poem, but the music is more that of form than of song. The music does not depend upon melting phrase or rhythm, nor upon sustained cantabile—no more than upon the evident strength or harsh dissonance. But still the imaginative form of the poem is musical in its arrangement, development, and control of theme and texture. . . . The resolution is achieved through a progress of transformation and recapitulation, through a system of inner references to what is the past history of any chosen moment in the developing form. . . . [Donne's] refusal to annihilate the past and the external in the progress of his poem can be taken as one sign of his musical imagination."

One might also add, as F. R. Leavis notes in *Revaluation: Tradition & Development in English Poetry*, that music seems to dominate as well the stanza forms which Donne uses: "In an age when music is for all classes an important part of daily life, when poets are, along with so large a proportion of their fellow-countrymen, musicians and write their lyrics to be sung, Donne uses in complete dissociation from music a stanza-form that proclaims the union of poetry and music." One might add further that not only the stanza forms, for there is only one stanza form which Donne uses more than once, but the title of the volume immediately set up comparisons with Tottel's earlier *Songs and Sonnets*. Clearly the mingling of long and short lines and the visual properties of Donne's poems owe much to what Miss Ing has shown to be the typographical innovations of that collection. Yet, if these effects are cultivated by Donne to replace the music that might have accompanied the poems, Hallett Smith rightly asserts in *Elizabethan Poetry* that "the lyrics of Donne . . . owe not so much to music . . . as they do to the rhythm of speech." The lyrics owe much, also, to the non-song tradition of the sixteenth-century lyric, including Tottel's collection, and the "plain diction" poems of Wyatt, Surrey, George Gascoigne, Raleigh, and Sir John Davies.

Certainly, if Donne's poems were ever intended to be songs, they were never intended as strophic songs. There are no corresponding phrases in each stanza to suggest their having gone to identical musical phrases, and the logical transitions between stanzas militate against emotional repetition. Moreover, the poems are too long for the kind of madrigal development which might have absorbed such imbalance. The possible exceptions are "Song: Sweetest love, I do not go," "The Message," and "The Bait," which in one manuscript are given as "Songs which were made to certain ayres which were made before." These songs, when compared with the lyrics of other songs of the 1590's, reveal much of the actual relationship of Donne with the musical composition theory of his time.

When compared, for example, to what Campion and Dowland were doing with the ayre, or even to what Wyatt's songs had achieved earlier, Donne's words for music represent a movement backward. This reversal occurs despite what his careful use of sounds indicates is a genuinely musical imagination. His pieces are generally more mellifluous than his nonmusical poems, but none shows any real ease in phrasing. "The Message" makes an attempt at parallel phrasing but fails to develop parallel emotions and results in musical imbalance. Fitting "Fit for no good sight, keep them still," "Keep it, for then 'tis none of mine," and "Or prove as false as thou art now" to the same expressive notes is difficult, if not impossible, if one adheres to the symptomatic emphasis which ideally is to obtain to each important word. Likewise, "Song: Sweetest love, I do not go" attempts no structure that might indicate that current principles of musical composition were in use. No parallel phrasing occurs, and its logical development forestalls emotional congruence. Both poems follow rhetorical patterns that put them closer to recitative than to strophic song. "The Bait," a parody of Christopher Marlowe's "The Passionate Shepherd to his Love," was no doubt intended to be sung to the music of that poem. It offers another attack on the exact union of words and music and suggests the sixteenth-century's use of musical parody more than its use of serious song. The practice of song parody which began in France with the setting of Clement Marot's Psalms to popular ditties spread early in the century to England and represented a complete antithesis to the efforts of the musical Academies. The poems seem to indicate that Donne found his own musical imagination constitutionally opposed to the current musical forms and used other means in his poetry to accomplish what he wanted.

Yet, by transforming musical techniques into oratorical purposes and abandoning the patterns of song, Donne did not abandon within his superstructure of Aristotelian rhetoric the growing attempts of music to define self-consciousness. As numerous critics have indicated, Donne's verse is marked first of all by an intense drive toward self-awareness. As Stein notes, "The themes of his art vary, but the distinguishing cause, insofar as one can identify it with a principal effect which is the distinguishing mark of his poetic achievement, is the drive for consciousness." In this drive, the shifting personae of *Songs and Sonnets* and more clearly of the *Elegies* become attempts to utilize the new concepts of a posteriori ideas to test predicaments and thereupon to correlate the beliefs of the various "I's" in order to see what is at work. The process is close to what George Herbert Mead was later in *Mind, Self and Society* to term "role taking" and "playing at a role." Instead of overt social behavior or conduct ("role playing"), role taking is a mental or cognitive or empathetic activity, a phase of symbolic process, by which a person momentarily pretends to himself that he is another person, projects himself into the perceptual field of another person, imaginatively "puts himself in the other's place," in order that he may get an insight into the other person's probable behavior in a given situation. This insight reveals, in turn, something of the projector's own nature. In "playing at a role," a person assumes a role which he cannot actually appropriate except in a make-believe, playful, fictitious, or fantasy form. Donne's playing at being an alchemist in "Love's Alchemy" is an example of it in action. The two processes should not be confused with living mythically, which is a form of "role playing."

Unquestionably these personae, which lead to the positing of a multiple ego, grew out of rhetorical practices like the *suasoriae* or dramatic speeches that had long been used in schoolrooms to persuade historical or even mythological personages to take or refrain from some well-known course of action. In practice, these personae require a large degree of the negative capability (and energy) involved in objectifying excitement which Cassirer has stressed. They also require a kind of skepticism, for, in order to get his audience to believe in what they say, the poet in the course of the poem must himself believe in the personae created by the various predicaments. Critics are generally agreed in seizing a line, "And the new philosophy calls all in doubt" (even itself), from "The First Anniversary" as the basis of Donne's skepticism, relegating it to Donne's youth and showing how it is resolved in his maturity. Yet, one might offer the idea of the mutability of all things within this sublunary sphere as well. Or, one might use Paul Valéry's concept of the artistic hero in "Introduction to the Method of Leonardo da Vinci" (1895) and insist that, in exploring the night of consciousness, every great artist discovers that the reality to which men are accustomed is but one solution out of many possible solutions. This pluralism can be reconciled only as the artist is able to divest objects of their peculiarities, and, at the same time, to sense what consciousness is apart from its objects, to reach, as it were, "the deep note of existence itself," where he can find a relationship between things whose laws of continuity escape ordinary perception. Donne in pursuing his course of pluralism and unity may have been merely following the same pattern.

The one matter of "true love" shows Donne's role taking in *Songs and Sonnets* to be far-ranging. "The Ecstasy," wherein the lovers' souls are "interinanimated," evinces a modified Neoplatonism. "The Good-morrow," wherein the love does not decay precisely because the lovers maintain a separate and equal tension between themselves, uses scholasticism. And "Love's Alchemy," wherein the marrying of bodies produces a marrying of minds, indulges in a concept of concinnity. Moreover, as A. J. Smith shows him to be in "The Ecstasy," Donne is likely to be eclectic within these various poems. The same role taking is true of his transient loves. In "Woman's Constancy," he attributes infidelity to the passage of time that makes lovers "not just those persons which they were." In "The Indifferent," he makes it a taste for variety, and, generally, he insists that true love requires more energy and attention than he is willing to give it. As Grierson concludes of Donne's overall attitude toward love in his Introduction to *Donne: Poetical Works:* "The dualism of body and soul he refused to accept as the absolute one to which medieval thought, influenced by Neo-Platonism, had tended. The body is not simply evil, the spirit good, sense a corrupter and misleader, the soul pure and heavenward aspiring. Man is body and soul, and neither can be complete without the other. To separate them absolutely is heresy alike in love and in religion." Still, from all Donne's discussions on serious matters, a reader concludes on the wit, the seriousness, the boastfulness, the extravagance, and the insecurity of the young Donne. The effect of these diverse positions, arranged to vacillate between true and transient loves, like the effects of the rapid changes of mood in baroque music does result in their turning upon themselves to reveal something of an individual. In this, they approximate some of the reversals and effects of the Elizabethan sonnet sequence.

Two techniques which Donne used in addition to predicaments contributed greatly to the self-consciousness of this role taking, or rather the selves-consciousness of it— colloquial diction and metaphysical imagery. To achieve the first, Donne abandoned the mellifluous diction of the Petrarchans and "used the wiry and often harsh rhythms of the spoken voice, as well as its informal, and often elliptical syntax." This Petrarchan diction, which, as critics have indicated, had "relied for its images mainly upon mythology and on natural objects," is replaced by "new sources such as law, science, philosophy, and the common places of urban life." Although Ben Jonson would have had Donne hanged for not keeping of accent, the "bad" scansion added to the colloquial impact, and with the device of emotionally charged language, gave to the poetry its sense of life.

The second of these techniques, the metaphysical image, has been the subject of much discussion. Rosemund Tuve sees it as "an image based simultaneously on a number of predicaments or common places in logic" and "framed with special subtlety," and she attaches it to Ramist logic. S. L. Bethell prefers to deal with it in terms of Aristotelian rhetoric, pointing out in "The Nature of Metaphysical Wit" that Ramist logic denies in its development the use of "sophisms" to persuade to right action. Establishing that Donne's enthymemes abound in sophisms and logical fallacies, he concludes that it seems unlikely that Donne would be following Ramus. Yet, since Donne quite often is persuading neither to right as in his attempts at seduction nor to beauty as in his portrayals of the grotesque, there is even within Bethell's argument room for doubt. Joseph A. Mazzeo summarizes the merits of the various positions in "Modern Theories of Metaphysical Poetry." He sees them falling basically into four camps. A first group, including C. S. Lewis, holds that the metaphysical image is a decadent exaggeration of Petrarch

and the troubadour tradition. Miss Tuve and her follow-
ers see it as an outgrowth of Ramist logic, which in turn
is an outgrowth of Aristotelian rhetoric. A third group,
led by Benedetto Croce, would have it a baroque phe-
nomenon which tried to parody or to purge Western
culture of its medievalism. Finally, a fourth group, in-
cluding Mario Praz and Austin Warren, holds that the
metaphysical image is related to the emblem, being of
the nature of the charade or riddle—the by-product of an
amusing, light-hearted, and perhaps perverse verbal and
pictorial game. Mazzeo warns that the image may owe
something to all of these theories, and the failure of critics
to distinguish the various functions of particular images
may be the proximate cause of their confusion.

Whatever the origins of the metaphysical image, critics
since the time of Samuel Johnson have agreed generally
upon its function in a metaphysical poem. It was a kind of
*discordia concors,* "a combination of dissimilar images,
or discovery of occult resemblances in things apparently
unlike." This view differs little from any of the four
prevalent theories of its origins. Yet, given the *locus,*
rather than causal connection between the dissimilar im-
ages, critics have disagreed as to whether or not the meta-
physical image was unified. In "The Life of Cowley"
(1779), Johnson sees it as dissociated: "The most hetero-
geneous ideas are yoked by violence together." In "John
Donne" (1899), Arthur Symons agrees: "Almost every
poem that he wrote is written on genuine inspiration, a
genuine personal inspiration, but most of his poems seem
to have been written before that personal inspiration has

had time to fuse itself with the poetic inspiration. It is always useful to remember Wordsworth's phrase of 'emotion recollected in tranquility,' for nothing so well defines that moment of crystallisation in which direct emotion of sensation deviates exquisitely into art."

Since the publication in 1921 of Eliot's enormously influential essay, "The Metaphysical Poets," the metaphysical image has been thought of as fused: "A thought to Donne was an experience; it modified his sensibility." Assuredly, between the disparate elements of the image a bond was, in fact, formed by the presence of the persona, as a bond had been, in fact, formed between the separate lovers in Ficino's concept of love; but one should seriously question whether the Romantic image which lies behind the statements of Symons and Eliot is relevant to Donne. Here the sociologist's distinction between "role playing" and "role taking" provides an insight. If, following Descartes, the Romantic image establishes the self on empiric grounds and has to deduce the object by projecting the self into it, by playing at it, the persona of Donne's poetry should know himself, according to Symons and Eliot, in the object. Yet, as Tuve remarks of Renaissance poets in general, "They characteristically point up the significance of groups of images in advance, or they use sharp epigrammatic summary statements at the close of a formally separate sequence." Hence, in Donne's poetry, where an intimate relationship between this object and the significance it enlists ought to occur, such a relationship does not exist. The objects of the poem occasion impersonal, abstractable, often proverbial presentations, and

Donne as often uses a fallacy of *secundum quid,* a shifting of terms, in order to make them relevant. The persona of the poem, rather than fusing experience, often merely extemporizes the *loci*—and that on the basis of analogy—where inner and outer experiences meet and might be correlated and leaves it to the reader to fuse them. What expenditure of energy there is is not in the sense that thought has become immediately the odor of a rose, but that the persona has functioned as a catalyst for the fusion. The persona, rather than the objects of the poem, becomes the object by which the poet knows himself.

In Donne, because this blatant technique of improvisation involves the reader, it emphasizes the wit and fantasy of the speaker rather than the truth of what is to follow. The resolution of these improvisations into an individual persona comes in *The Divine Poems,* when the sublunary changes resolve into an underlying imitation of Christ, referred to by Donne in "La Carona" as "white sincerity." In these poems, as Louis L. Martz indicates in *The Poetry of Meditation,* the technique of predicaments takes on resemblances to the composition of places as explained in *The Spiritual Exercises.* According to Ignatius, "in contemplation or meditation on visible matters, such as the contemplation of Christ our Lord, Who is visible, the composition will be to see with the eyes of the imagination the corporeal place where the thing I wish to contemplate is found." As St. Bonaventure had explained earlier in his *Meditations on the Life of Christ,* this contemplation generally of the Humanity of Christ was imperfect as compared with the contemplation of the majesty of God or of the heavenly courts. The contemplator takes part in the life of Christ, who becomes the *locus* of Christological history, but he in no way assumes Christ's life. In this role, Christ provides the mediation between inner and outer experiences of time, and the mediator Donne, not daring to move his dim eyes in any direction other than Christ, tries to discover for himself the true law of continuity by which his multiple selves might be resolved. Whereas in the secular poems Donne seems to have imagined the scenes before the poems began, one senses that Donne is here composing his scenes within the poem. As a result, they are more descriptive, pictorial, Petrarchan (hence Ciceronian), and of a piece than the early poems, but there are signs that a singular will has struggled fiercely to impose itself upon their subject matter. An almost satanic wilfullness intrudes. Yet one senses, too, that the person of Christ who acts as a catalyst for Donne's understanding of the inner and outer realms of Christianity is not different from the more finite personae of the secular lyrics, but a more perfectly realized example of these personae.

The singular will of Donne's "sincere" ego, which results from a mythic confrontation, is religious in purpose and contrasts well with the "normative" ego which, at the same time, was evolving in the poetry of Ben Jonson. This normative ego emerged as an overt response to contemporary life and succeeded later in dominating neo-classical poetry. It combined social need and social acceptance into a public statement, determining by decorum the proper stance and degree of emotion. Nowhere is this determination more evident than in Jonson's elegy, "On My First Daughter":

> Here lies, to each her parents' ruth,
> Mary, the daughter of their youth:
> Yet, all heavens' gifts, being heavens' due,
> It makes the father less to rue.
> At six months' end, she parted hence
> With safety of her innocence;
> Whose soul heaven's Queen, (whose name she bears)
> In comfort of her mother's tears,
> Hath placed amongst her virgin-train;
> Where, while that severed doth remain,
> This grave partakes the fleshly birth—
> Which cover lightly, gentle earth.

In it, Jonson seems more passionately concerned with his daughter's having preserved her innocence than with her having missed the joys of childhood. He searches accordingly for an expression of grief which is proper to all deaths rather than allowing the particular closeness of his daughter's situation to warp him here into excess. In "Ben Jonson's Lyric Poetry," Ralph Walker makes this "insistence on the classic and permanent virtues of restraint, simplicity, decorum and good workmanship" a valuable "corrective to the bad effect which such an individual style as Donne's might have had on its imitators." He goes on to note that "if his [Jonson's] lyrics have a frigid and translucent beauty like that of a crystal cameo, they are like a cameo also in their unashamed avowal of the carver's hand."

But to see how restrained this first elegy is, one need

only compare it to an elegy for a nonrelative, "Epitaph on Elizabeth, L.H.":

> Wouldst thou hear what man can say
> In a little? Reader, stay.
> Underneath this stone doth lie
> As much beauty as could die,
> Which in life did harbor give
> To more virtue than doth live.
> If, at all, she had a fault,
> Leave it buried in this vault.
> One name was Elizabeth;
> The other—let it sleep with death.
> Fitter, where it died, to tell,
> Than that it lived at all. Farewell.

Again, a frigid classicism obtains.

The impartiality of Jonson, which can be seen in these two elegies, becomes his social equivalent to Donne's mythic self-definition. With it, he tries to assert a particular social demeanor on which he would like to rest his particular identity. The effort has led to admiration such as that registered by Williams: "Jonson's triumph is his style. It is the first in English lyric poetry that is really capable of comprehending the extreme range and diversity of human experience, without falsifying that experience or doing violence to it." "It was Jonson," C. V. Wedgwood adds in *Seventeenth-Century English Literature,* "who shattered the older foreign moulds in which English verse had formed, not—as Donne was more subtly doing—by a different approach to the subject, but by spilling and pouring into English verse the antique vintages of Greece and

Rome until the old mould cracked with the pressure. He left Italy and the Renaissance on one side and dreamed of Catullus, Horace, and Anacreon." This desertion of Italian rhetoric and patterns of eccentric behavior for impartiality fostered a generalized diction that lent itself easily to contemporary song theory. The diction did not have the individual excesses of Donne. Rather it sought the stoical "manly carriage" which Campion admired in *A Book of Ayres*.

By modulating between the expressions of Donne's "sincere" ego, the "dramatic" or "multiple" ego, and Jonson's "normative" ego, the seventeenth-century lyric was left to refine itself as a vehicle for self-consciousness. Many of its successes and failures stem from this modulation. In the sense that any decision on persona required an accurate judgment of aesthetic distance, the lyricist had then to arrive—as does the modern fiction writer in regard to point of view—at a means for selecting the proper distance and for justifying the particular changes in distance that might be necessary. For example, the intimacy of the sincere ego made it ideal for subjective, religious meditation. But, when one had to shift from it to a normative ego, as George Herbert had done in "The Collar" and Andrew Marvell in many poems, one had to rely upon a device either of dialogue or of irony. Like the interplay of Astrophel and Petrarch, the interplay of these egos tended to give the work what tension it contained. Sometimes, as in sections of Henry King's "The Exequy," the shift did not achieve a tension. Then the reader was caught up in the disparity. He found the poem fragmenting before his mind's eye, the separation of inner and outer realities complete, and the transformations which the sixteenth-century lyric underwent to achieve its structures of self-consciousness defeated. In this defeat, the seventeenth century moved to more overt and specialized forms of self-analyses in the autobiography.

When in 1921 *Metaphysical Lyrics & Poems of the Seventeenth Century* appeared, the bond between the sixteenth-century views of self-consciousness and the modern poet was clearly established in Eliot's "The Metaphysical Poets." Building upon both the specific interest in Donne which had been massing since Alexander Grosart's edition of the poems in 1872 and a general fin-de-siècle interest in the processes of thought, Eliot forged what was to be over the next decades the dominant view of the poet. Edmund Wilson described the view in *Axel's Castle* as a "new technique, at once laconic, quick, and precise" that represents the "interplay of perception and reflection." It cut corners and moved not by logical stages, but, like Eliot's view of Donne, as live thoughts in live brains. To a generation who somehow felt they were being cheated of their feelings by mass-production methods, it suggested a romantic step backward toward a mode of "a direct sensuous apprehension of thought, or a recreation of thought into feeling" and a sensibility which, according to Eliot, sometime during the seventeenth century had "dissociated." As he wrote in "The Metaphysical Poets," "When a poet's mind is perfectly equipped for its work, it is constantly amalgamating disparate experience; the ordinary man's experience is chaotic, irregular, fragmentary. The latter falls in love, or reads Spinoza, and these two experiences have nothing to do with each other, or with the noise of the typewriter or the smell of cooking; in the mind of the poet these experiences are always forming new wholes." In "Donne in Our Time," Eliot was to modify radically this position on Donne's sensibility, but to far less effect. Omitting from the second essay the romantic sense of a past somehow richer and fuller than the present which had been part of the attraction of the first essay, he asserts, "One reason why Donne has appealed so powerfully to the recent time is that there is in his poetry hardly any attempt at organization; rather a puzzled and humorous shuffling of the pieces; and we are inclined to read our more conscious awareness of the apparent irrelevance and unrelatedness of things into the mind of Donne."

By the time of this assertion, a generation of poets had already taken the disenchantment of their dissociated sensibilities and, by an emulation of Donne's technique as described by Eliot and modified by other critics, sought under critics like I. A. Richards to fuse their world visions into new "unified" sensibilities. These fusions might be possible, they thought, through discovering the "wit" of Donne, that kind of *discordia concors* which Johnson had denied, but which through a utilization of texture, paradox, ambiguity, logic, dramatic and ironic stances, and mythic structures might combine dissimilar images or discover occult resemblances in things apparently unlike. As Robert Lowell indicates in "Prose Genius in Verse," the problem of the modern poet became one of making

Spinoza and love fit together. This would be accomplished by "repoeticizing," by a contemplative transcendence similar to that achieved in Donne's final poems: "Under this dying-to-the-world discipline the stiffest and most matter of fact items were repoeticized—quotations from John of the Cross, usury, statistics, conversations and newspaper clippings." Earlier he had remarked in "A Note" that the greatness and genius of Gerard Manley Hopkins lay in his ability through contemplation "to use most of his interests and experiences in his poetry." The remarks are echoed in Eliot's statement in "Milton" of the intentions of his own generation "that the subject-matter and the imagery of poetry should be extended to topics and objects related to the life of a modern man or woman; that we were to seek the non-poetic, to seek even material refractory to transmutation into poetry, and words and phrases which had not been used in poetry before."

In his book on Donne, Stein summarizes the four stylistic elements which through Eliot may have most influenced modern assumptions about poetry: a tendency to obscurity; a license to make individual raids on modern nonpoetic experience; an emphasis in verse on "talk"; and a richness of imagery. In a *Paris Review* interview, Lowell sheds special light on the way the first two elements affected both his poetry and that of Allen Tate: "We both liked rather formal, difficult poems, and we were reading particularly the Sixteenth and Seventeenth centuries. . . . [In imitating these poets] we wanted our formal patterns to seem a hardship and something that we couldn't rattle off easily." Yet, formality was not enough. To rescue the

171

new poetry from culture, invention was also desirable, as he had shown in "Prose Genius in Verse" and "A Note." It was not only proof of *discordia concors* in one's work, but would as well prevent the divorcement of self from modern experience which one's simply using these poets as vehicles for defining the tenor of a modern self would effect. "Poets of my generation," Lowell goes on to note, "and particularly younger ones . . . write a very musical, difficult poem with tremendous skill." "Yet," he remarks, "the writing seems divorced from culture somehow. It's become too much something specialized that can't handle experience."

This unforeseen reduction in the poet's ability to handle experience which was in part a result of Eliot's essay on Donne was also in part a consequence of several impulses having nothing to do with Eliot. Foremost among them is the inversion of Castiglione which Oscar Wilde makes in "The Decay of Lying" (1889) and which extends through most fin-de-siècle aesthetics. For Wilde, as it had been for Renaissance critics, art is a false world, independent of life, "and develops purely on its own lines." But whereas for Castiglione an impulse, indicating man's free will, stylized both art and life, for Wilde, "Life imitates Art far more than Art imitates Life. This results . . . from the fact that the self-conscious aim of Life is to find expression, and that Art offers it certain beautiful forms through which it may realize that energy." The possible forms of that art have already been exhausted and only a process of their proliferation through metaphor remains. The predetermination implicit in this process can be evaded only by an act of will which, having once turned life into art on the basis of previous art, then destroys that which it has created as proof of its freedom. In the terminology of the day, attributable to Friedrich Nietzsche's *The Birth of Tragedy* (1872), it was the tension of Apollonian and Dionysian states, each of which successively gave rise to the other.

In Eliot's interpretation of Donne, he had inadvertently contributed to the continuance of this inversion and its predetermination as well as sought to expand the range of poetry by insisting that Donne had filtered his experiences through a singular rather than a multiple persona. Thinking mainly that through a Wordsworthian device of recollection more varied and variable material could be worked into poetry, he had failed to note the real method of Donne's absorption of nonpoetic experience. The personae of the Donne poem did not fuse inner and outer realities into a single impression; they located these realities by becoming their indissoluble bond. The spontaneity with which they worked required the cooperation of the audience who expected mental agility, not truth. The partnership had more resemblance to Falstaff's getting out of the lie of having faced "eleven buckram men grown out of two" in *Henry IV, Part I,* by pleading that it was not for him "to kill the heir apparent" than it had to any interiorization. Thus, as in Eliot the process of metaphysical imagery gives way to a metaphor of Donne, in his followers, extemporizing like Donne's becomes not self-expression, but a channeling of ego into Donnean echoes. In such terms, as their strong lines remained "talk," they became decorative talk, circumscribed by the limits of Donne as Renaissance Latin had been circumscribed by the limits of Cicero, and because of the pictorialism of the lines' having to evoke the vehicles both for a poetic pose and for the objectifications of subjective states, they required for their success an energy far in excess of that originally used by Donne.

In accounting for Theodore Roethke's many breakdowns in *The Glass House,* Allan Seager focuses particularly upon the excessive energy required by such proliferations of metaphor. Showing how Richards' statement in *Principles of Literary Criticism* that the "availability of his past experience is the first characteristic of the poet" demanded from Roethke "a persistent attention to his own past," Seager goes on to note: "His history, as he saw it, was one of losses, betrayal, shame, many fears, and guilt. To immerse himself in these, to force them into images or to contemplate them until they became images that he, hence others, could accept, and to find a suitable diction for them was not only taxing but may have been dangerous." Seager then clarifies his view by citing statements made by Roethke's "best" psychiatrist, Dr. William Hoffer: "I think his troubles were merely the running expenses he paid for being his kind of poet." "Given the intensity of his vocation and the emotional costs of his method of work," Seager explains, "Dr. Hoffer seems to be saying that Ted's troubles were inevitable." Throughout much of the book Seager shows how the image of W. B. Yeats was the instrument of Roethke's objectification—Roethke transforming not only his own poetic style but his personal relationships to echoes of Yeats's style and life. In one point, he quotes the description of one of Roethke's students to show how, in the manner of Wordsworth and Rainer Maria Rilke, Roethke's metaphysical fusions were a result of his pursuit of the Romantic image, of a burrowing into objects until they had become him and their expression became an expression of his consciousness.

Closely related to Eliot's failure to depict accurately the nature of the energy with which Donne poeticized experience was another: Eliot failed to emphasize the skepticism which enabled Donne to write of himself with such endurance. The result of this misunderstanding has been a quantity of poetry in which the poet like Erysichthon tears at the body of his metaphoric image of himself until he has eaten it completely. One has merely to go through the "self-destructive" imagery of a poet like Dylan Thomas or more recently Galway Kinnell to verify how this Dionysian process ends in a disgust which does carry into life. The rejection of this multiple persona, or its perception and then the delay in its acceptance, may well have been due to an absolutism which motivated the generation of writers after Eliot. In "The New Criticism and the Democratic Tradition," Robert Gorham Davis has pointed out that the related terms of honor among these writers were authority, absolutes, dogma, and truth, and that their terms of rejection and contempt were liberalism, naturalism, scientism, individualism, progress, Protestantism, pragmatism, and personality. Under their management, the skepticism which had been part of Donne became not a method of trying out their own awarenesses of self, but a subterfuge for promoting their beliefs to an otherwise hostile and brainwashed audience. Their partnership was not one of Falstaffian high jinks but one of sinister deception. It was justifiable upon the grounds which allowed Aristotle to permit a rhetorician to use false arguments for good aims. As Leslie A. Fiedler remarks in "The Believing Poet and the Infidel Reader," the allegiance required that writer and reader share in an indirection which forced the writer into the ambiguities of translation and of satire as well as into the dramatic and the baroque. In translation, the writer described "the flora and fauna of a new country with only the terms on a list prepared by one who had never been there." Because of the dual illusions of reality, despite a common language, no real common ground between writer and reader could exist. Rather the writer wrote for an initiated few who could make the proper substitutions. Within this general ambiguity lay the ambiguity of satire, which distorted what was to be accepted, not what was to be despised. The dramatic offered the writer a device for evading responsibility by attributing his statements to someone else. Finally, the use of the baroque, by making the disjunction of center and surface its rationale, allowed complication to become the essence of pattern. One need not resolve his disjunctions. Yet, rather than presenting an alternative to the situation, Fiedler's own terminology of "ambiguity" betrays his indebtedness to an inner absolutism—a sincere ego against which ambiguity can be tried.

This complicity of believing writer and infidel reader

of which Fiedler writes permits the reader to insist "the poet's skills, his music, or his honest eye" is "the source of pleasure," or "a trifle condescendingly, the unbelieving reader will confide that a particular 'false and partial' view is, at the moment, 'useful.'" Meanwhile, the writer will insist that he has both done his duty by propagating "truth" and avoided catering to a mass ignorance. Thus, while the reader is avidly looking for the heresies in the writer's orthodoxy, the writer is smugly wallowing in having put something over on his readers. Under such conditions of gamesmanship, where the "self" must be known beforehand so that it may be disguised and where its disguises prevent any new knowledge of self, it is only a matter of time before both writer and reader tire of evasion, and, as with changes of fashion, the pendulum swing away from the equivocal toward the sincere, and finally the confessional poem emerge.

As early as 1935, William Carlos Williams prepares for such an emergence in a letter to Marianne Moore: "But to me a book is somewhat of a confessional. It is just because I do not say things that-I-would-say that I must write them." In 1947, in his review of *Lord Weary's Castle,* Fiedler notes, "In the more serious lyric, we have come more and more to expect the poet's personal voice, to demand that he really subscribes to what he avows. But Lowell shies away from the intimate confession he senses may be unwelcome, welcomes the obliquy of the dramatic, and especially its illusion of objectivity." So, in 1959, when Lowell's *Life Studies* proved to be what M. L. Rosenthal was to call "poetry as confession," it was the completion of a process which had begun long before. The "counterfeits" which had occupied the characters in *Henry IV, Part I* had to be got rid of if honest kingship was to take hold. In "Finding a Poem," W. D. Snodgrass describes the process of their removal in his work: "It seems to me that the poets of our generation—those of us who have gone so far in criticism and analysis that we cannot ever turn back and be innocent again, who have such extensive resources for disguising ourselves from ourselves—that our only hope as artists is to continually ask ourselves, 'Am I writing what I *really* think? Not what is acceptable; not what my favorite intellectual would think in this situation; not what I wish I felt. Only what I cannot help thinking.' " He admits that he is "left, then, with a very old-fashioned measure of a poem's worth—the depth of its sincerity."

Still, if the lyric since its divorce from music functions as a vehicle for the "kingship" of consciousness, it encounters new dangers as a mode of confession. Wright cautions: "As everything within the poem comes more and more to be a reproduction of actual things and people outside it, and the 'I' becomes increasingly the poet himself, the poem runs the risk of losing the peculiar properties of poems." This risk of losing the peculiar properties of poems seems to be the problem of the lyric since *Life Studies,* when Lowell, who had earlier espoused the Eliot view of Donne and the New Criticism's stance of complicity, shifted into sincerity. As Joseph Bennett remarked in "Two Americans, a Brahmin and the Bourgeoisie," the book was "a collection of lazily recollected and somewhat snobbish memoirs . . . more suited as an appendix to some snobbish society magazine . . . than a purposeful work." In his Introduction to Sylvia Plath's *Ariel,* Lowell seems himself to have become aware of the dangers: "Everything in these poems is personal, confessional, felt, but the manner of feeling is controlled hallucination, the autobiography of a fever. . . . Yet it is too much, her art's immortality is life's disintegration. . . . These poems are playing Russian roulette with six cartridges in the cylinder, a game of 'chicken,' the wheels of both cars locked and unable to swerve."

In the light of such statements, regaining the peculiar properties of poems should be the intent of the contemporary lyric, but this might not mean a return to the problems of the sincere ego and "the believing poet and the infidel reader." Rather it might mean a return to the method of imagery and skepticism of Donne as it was understood by the Renaissance and as more recently it has been understood by sociologists and psychologists and even by Eliot's contemporaries—Ezra Pound, Joyce, and Valéry. Pound presumably discovered the need for a multiple ego through the writings of Robert Browning, and Valéry certainly through the life of Leonardo da Vinci. As Mead has indicated, there are two stages in the full development of the self. In the first, "the individual's self is constituted simply by an organization of the particular attitudes of other individuals toward himself and toward one another in the specific social acts in which he participates with them." In the second, "that self is constituted not only by an organization of these particular individual attitudes, but also by an organization of the social attitudes of the generalized other or the social group as a whole to which he belongs." In his memoir on *Gaudier-Brzeska,* Pound discusses his own role taking:

In the "search for oneself," in the search for "sincere self-expression," one gropes, one finds some seeming verity. One says "I am" this, that, or the other, and with the words scarcely uttered one ceases to be that thing.

I began this search for the real in a book called *Personae,* casting off, as it were, complete masks of the self in each poem. I continued in long series of translations, which were but more elaborate masks.

Wright comments on the success of this role taking that "much like Tiresias in *The Waste Land,* the persona of *The Cantos* serves as a point of fusion for all the characters in the poem, and not only for the characters but for the scenes and civilizations as well." But rather than "a point of fusion," it is clear that the persona of *Cantos* acts as a point of convergence. This convergence, which embraces the contradictions of both the particularized and the generalized other, serves to create a fuller awareness of self than that possible under the more limited self of Eliot. Likewise, in *Ulysses,* Joyce has Leopold Bloom in the nighttown scene undergo a series of transformations and guises as an illustration of his multiple ego, and in *Finnegans Wake* extends the process to HCE and his wife. Valéry's statement in "Introduction to the Method of Leonardo da Vinci" that it is only "at the deep note of existence itself" that this pluralism is reconciled has already been noted. More recently this concept of a multiple ego has served to develop the images of self in poems like William Carlos Williams' *Paterson* and John Berryman's *77 Dream Songs* and *His Toy, His Dream, His Rest,* demonstrating that at least the structures for the tension between the multiple ego and a fully developed self are alive and viable and require no great alterations in a reader's habits of thought. In *His Toy, His Dream, His Rest,* Berryman notes: "The poem then, whatever its wide cast of characters, is essentially about an imaginary character (not the poet, not me) named Henry, a white American in early middle age sometimes in blackface, who has suffered an irreversible loss and talks about himself sometimes in the first person, sometimes in the third, sometimes even in the second; he has a friend, never named, who addresses him as Mr Bones and variants thereof." Certainly, with such a view of persona, the persona of the *Cantos,* seen like the personae of Donne's *Songs and Sonnets* as forming a locus of convergence rather than of fusion, loses much of his insurmountable complexity, and a reader might in this circumstance begin to understand and enjoy the work.

In the evolving search in the sixteenth century for instruments of consciousness, one can thus see what the dissociation of words and music eventually meant, not, only for music and literature but also for the psychology infusing both forms. Music and words found themselves at the start of the century in a close union that extended back to a pre-Christian era and was partly the result of a primitive form of musical notation which could not allow notes to be phrased, interpreted, or measured without reference to their accompanying words. The union continued, aided by the writings of the Church Fathers, who like Augustine placed both music and words under the broad definition of language (*verba*) and showed that they interpreted the same reality (*res*). Later, in Boethius' *De institutione musica,* but still under the influence of this *res-verba* connection, music (including words) separated into three general categories: *musica mundana, musica humana,* and *in instrumentis constitua.* So separated, music made its appeals to the soul, the body politic, and material reality. In all three divisions, its function was the restoration or institution of a harmony through a means of sympathetic vibration; in its highest form, *musica mundana,* the right proportions of the notes were thought to be able to put man in tune with the music of the spheres.

This patristic view of language invaded the Christian approach to serious secular literature, which dating from the Stoics had been interpreted along allegorical lines. Divided by the Church similarly into three categories— the spiritual, the moral, and the literal—literature was made to correspond to a division that St. Paul was thought to have made. In the ninth century, a fourth category was inserted between the literal and moral senses, and interpretations of serious nonmusical literature remained thus divided into the Renaissance. In extending this threefold interpretation to the body of Christian literature, Augustine in *De doctrina Christiana* tried to reconcile a Ciceronian rhetoric of humble, moderate, and grand styles to a basically Platonic end in Truth. He insisted that the humble style be used in teaching great things, the moderate for praise and blame in regard to great things, and the grand for persuading the reluctant with regard to great things. Although not always accepted by writers, his reconciliation dominated both musical and nonmusical Christian poetry in England to about 1500. At that point, under the impact of humanism, the direction begun in fourteenth-century treatises on music to disregard the philosophical bases of music and to deal only with the techniques of musical embellishment, and similarly in treatises on rhetoric, the tendency to encourage embellishment along the lines of Cicero, Quintilian, and Petrarch, encroached upon the close union of music and words, more and more splitting the forms apart and sending the lyrics into frameworks which over the centuries had been built for the purpose of handling nonmusical, serious, secular literature.

As Burckhardt long ago pointed out in *The Civilization of the Renaissance in Italy,* individualism became a dominant impulse of this Renaissance humanism, and both music and lyrics in the sixteenth century provided vehicles for the self-consciousness to which it was allied. The new demands required a music that was more rhetorical so as to place scenes before the eyes of its hearers, that was simpler so that one could sing and be understood, and that was chromatic so as to be expressive of man's emotions rather than of some divine arithmetic. Finally, in executing these demands, music established its own illusion of reality and could stand by itself. In gaining this independence of words, music's significative systems and forms were altered to become more fully expressive of man's range of self-definition. At the same time, the demands which let music become independent of words and productive of its own forms of self-definition, increasingly asked lyric poetry to be social rather than religious, and personally rather than typically expressive. New aesthetic distances emerged and by 1600 it was clear that in England lyric poetry had formed an equally independent system. The two systems had taken dissociated paths that would prevent their easily coming together again. John Donne, who wrote without music and based his techniques upon rhetoric, established the frames for self-discovery in the early seventeenth century. Ben Jonson, as Miss Wedgwood indicates, contributed to these frames by throwing "down for future English poets the restrictive barriers of Italian rhetoric," setting the poets "to take their models where they chose, and to put their trust in the natural qualities of their own melodious and voluble tongue," and by delineating the normative persona of the century. After Donne and Jonson, the perfect union of words and music disappeared; song meter and verbal rhythm, as they remained connected, became differentiated into formal aria and narrative recitative. As William Carlos Williams perceptively remarks, in a letter to Pound (1932), of the effects of the dissociation on subsequent lyric poetry as a vehicle for self-consciousness: "Whereas formerly the music which accompanied the words amplified, certified and released them, today the words we write, failing a patent music, have become the music itself, and the understanding of the individual (presumed) is now that which used to be the words." This shift from music and words to music and self-understanding and words and self-understanding becomes the overall inner consistency in the structural transformations undergone by the English lyric in the sixteenth century.

# References

❧ *Chapter One: Res-Verba* Relations

*Page*

2. Neal Ward Gilbert, *Renaissance Concepts of Method* (New York, 1960), pp. 66, 71.

   E. H. Gombrich, *Art and Illusion* (2d ed.; New York, 1961), p. 11.

3. Joel E. Spingarn, *Literary Criticism in the Renaissance* (Harbinger Books, 1963), pp. 37, 99.

4. St. Augustine, "On Music," tr. R. C. Taliaferro, in *The Fathers of the Church,* ed. Ludwig Schopp et al. (New York, 1947), IV, 179.

5. Spingarn, p. 6.

9. Robert M. Grant, *A Short History of the Interpretation of the Bible* (London, 1965), p. 95.

15. Clement as quoted in Gretchen Finney, *Musical Backgrounds for English Literature: 1580–1650* (New Brunswick, 1961), p. 56.

Dante Alighieri, "De vulgari eloquentia," *A Translation of the Latin Works,* ed. A. G. Ferrers Howell (London, 1940), pp. 70–71.

16. George T. Wright, *The Poet in the Poem* (Berkeley, 1960), pp. 30–31.

   John Williams, Preface, *English Renaissance Poetry* (Anchor Books, 1963), pp. ix–x.

17. Wright, p. 31.

   Gilbert, p. 69.

19. Pierre de Ronsard, *A Brief on the Art of French Poetry,* tr. J. H. Smith, in *The Great Critics,* ed. James Harry Smith and Edd Winfield Parks (3d ed.; New York, 1951), p. 184.

   Fracastoro as quoted in Spingarn, p. 31.

21. Rossell Hope Robbins, Introduction, *Secular Lyrics of the XIVth and XVth Centuries* (Oxford, 1952), pp. xxiv, lii–liii.

23. E. M. W. Tillyard, *The English Renaissance: Fact or Fiction?* (London, 1952), pp. 35–36.

25. Brian Trowell, "The Early Renaissance," in *The Pelican History of Music,* ed. Alec Robertson and Denis Stevens (Penguin Books, 1963), II, 81.

26. E. D. Mackerness, *A Social History of English Music* (Toronto, 1964), p. 41.

28. M. J. C. Hodgart, "Medieval Lyrics and the Ballads," in *The Age of Chaucer,* ed. Boris Ford (Penguin Books, 1954), p. 164.

   Robbins, p. liv.

29. Albert Seay, *Music in the Medieval World* (Englewood Cliffs, 1965), p. 129.

30. Erasmus as quoted in James A. Froude, *Life and Letters of Erasmus* (New York, 1896), pp. 122–123.

31. Aaron Copland, *Music and Imagination* (Mentor Books, 1959), p. 12.
32. John Stevens, *Music & Poetry in the Early Tudor Court* (London, 1961), p. 38.
   Wilfrid Mellers, "Words and Music in Elizabethan England," in *The Age of Shakespeare*, ed. Boris Ford (Penguin Books, 1955), pp. 390, 389.
33. *Ibid.*, p. 402.
34. M. C. Boyd, *Elizabethan Music and Musical Criticism* (2d ed.; Philadelphia, 1962), p. 62.
35. Catherine Ing, *Elizabethan Lyrics* (London, 1951), p. 88. Williams, p. ix.
36. Rosemund Tuve, *Elizabethan and Metaphysical Imagery* (Chicago, 1947), p. 19.
   Mellers, p. 403.

🍁 *Chapter Two:* The Message and the Medium

*Page*
38. Irving Singer, *The Nature of Love: Plato to Luther* (New York, 1966), p. xii.
39. J. W. Lever, *The Elizabethan Love Sonnet* (London, 1956), p. 10.
40. Lisle John, *The Elizabethan Sonnet Sequence* (New York, 1938), p. 43.
41. C. S. Lewis, *The Allegory of Love* (Oxford, 1936), p. 17.
45. Elyot as quoted in Maurice Valency, *In Praise of Love* (New York, 1958), p. 142.
   John Hollander, *The Untuning of the Sky* (Princeton, 1961), p. 90.
48. Sidney Lee, Introduction, *Elizabethan Sonnets* (Westminster, 1904), I, xxvii.

52. Hugh M. Richmond, *The School of Love* (Princeton, 1964), p. 238.

A. J. Smith, "The Metaphysic of Love," *Review of English Studies*, n.s. IX (1958), 363.

53. Ebreo as quoted in Smith, pp. 365, 366.

55. John Williams, Preface, *English Renaissance Poetry* (Anchor Books, 1963), pp. xiii–xiv.

Sergio Baldi, *Sir Thomas Wyatt*, tr. F. T. Prince (London, 1961), p. 33.

57. W. H. Auden, "John Skelton," in *The Great Tudors*, ed. Katherine Garvin (London, 1935), p. 62.

58. Williams, pp. ix–x.

61. Philip Henderson, Introduction, *The Complete Poems of John Skelton* (London, 1948), p. xxix.

H. A. Mason, *Humanism and Poetry in the Early Tudor Court* (London, 1959), p. 174.

62. Maurice Evans, *English Poetry in the Sixteenth Century* (2d ed.; New York, 1967), p. 71.

63. E. M. W. Tillyard, *The English Renaissance: Fact or Fiction?* (London, 1952), p. 49.

64. R. G. Cox, "A Survey of Literature from Donne to Marvell," in *From Donne to Marvell*, ed. Boris Ford (Penguin Books, 1956), p. 60.

Mark Van Doren, *Introduction to Poetry* (New York, 1968), p. 37.

65. Catherine Ing, *Elizabethan Lyrics* (London, 1951), p. 141.

67. Baldi, p. 22.

68. *Ibid.*, pp. 18–19, 22–23.

69. Evans, p. 81.

70. *Ibid.*, p. 77.

C. S. Lewis, *English Literature in the Sixteenth Century* (Oxford, 1954), p. 231.

*Page*

74. Sidney Lee, Introduction, *Elizabethan Sonnets* (Westminster, 1904), I, xliv.

75. Thomas Bergin, Introduction, in *Lyric Poetry of the Italian Renaissance,* ed. L. R. Lind (New Haven, 1954), p. xxiv.

77. Scaliger as quoted in Izora Scott, *Controversies over the Imitation of Cicero* (New York, 1910), p. 51.

78. Paul Oskar Kristeller, *Renaissance Thought* (Harper Torchbooks, 1961), p. 71.
Roger Ascham, "Of Imitation," in *Elizabethan Critical Essays,* ed. G. Gregory Smith (London, 1904), I, 3.

81. E. M. W. Tillyard, *The Poetry of Sir Thomas Wyatt* (London, 1929), p. 22.
Ascham, I, 31.

82. *Ibid.,* 7.

83. Ascham as quoted in Wilbur Samuel Howell, *Logic and Rhetoric in England, 1500–1700* (New York, 1961), p. 173.
Jacob Burckhardt, *The Civilization of the Renaissance in Italy,* tr. S. G. C. Middlemore (New York, 1954), pp. 100–101.

84. Kristeller, p. 20.
Charles Homer Haskins, *The Renaissance of the Twelfth Century* (Cambridge, Mass., 1939), pp. 11–12.
Douglas Bush, *The Renaissance and English Humanism* (Toronto, 1939), p. 38.

85. Erwin Panofsky, *Studies in Iconology* (Harper Torchbooks, 1962), p. 27.

86. Ernst Cassirer, *The Individual and the Cosmos in Renaissance Philosophy*, tr. Mario Domandi (Harper Torchbooks, 1963), p. 134.

87. Burckhardt, p. 101.

James M. Osborn, Introduction, *The Autobiography of Thomas Whythorne* (Oxford, 1962), p. xi.

89. Anna Robeson Burr, *The Autobiography* (Boston, 1909), p. 205.

91. Paul Oskar Kristeller, *Renaissance Thought II* (Harper Torchbooks, 1965), p. 153.

92. E. E. Lowinsky, *Secret Chromatic Art in the Netherlands Motet*, tr. Carl Buchman (New York, 1946), pp. 21, 108, 98.

93. John Hollander, *The Untuning of the Sky* (Princeton, 1961), p. 199.

Charles Garside, Jr., *Zwingli and the Arts* (New Haven, 1966), p. 67.

94. Ernst Troeltsch, *Protestantism and Progress*, tr. W. Montgomery (Beacon Paperbacks, 1958), p. 168.

Thomas Whythorne, *The Autobiography of Thomas Whythorne*, pp. 205, 204.

95. *Ibid.*, p. 203.

Peter LeHuray, *Music and the Reformation in England, 1549–1660* (New York, 1967), p. 135.

96. *Ibid.*, p. 141.

97. Gustave Reese, *Music in the Renaissance* (2d ed.; New York, 1959), pp. 819–820.

Joseph Kerman, *The English Madrigal* (New York, 1962), p. 12.

98. Thomas Wilson as quoted in Howell, pp. 18–19.

Aristotle, *The Rhetoric of Aristotle*, tr. Lane Cooper (New York, 1960), p. 119.

192

Rosemund Tuve, *Elizabethan and Metaphysical Imagery* (Chicago, 1947), p. 343.

99. *Ibid.*, pp. 334, 335.

Cusanus as quoted in Cassirer, p. 130.

100. Paul H. Kocher, *Science and Religion in Elizabethan England* (San Marino, Cal., 1953), p. 293.

Patrick Cruttwell, "Physiology and Psychology in Shakespeare's Age," *Journal of the History of Ideas*, XII (1951), 87.

101. David Kalstone, *Sidney's Poetry* (Cambridge, Mass., 1965), p. 108.

103. *Ibid.*, p. 135.

104. Sir Philip Sidney, "An Apology for Poetry," in Smith, I, 195.

105. *Ibid.*, 159, 168, 196.

Sidney as quoted in Harold White, *Plagiarism and Imitation during the English Renaissance* (Cambridge, Mass., 1935), p. 63.

Sidney in Smith, I, 201.

106. White, p. 79.

107. Sidney in Smith, I, 201.


🍁 *Chapter Four:* New Alliances

*Page*

111. Friedrich Blume, *Renaissance and Baroque Music,* tr. M. D. Herter Norton (New York, 1967), p. 105.

Rachel Bespaloff, *On the Iliad,* tr. Mary McCarthy (Harper Torchbooks, 1962), pp. 73–74.

113. George Puttenham, in *Elizabethan Critical Essays,* ed. G. Gregory Smith (London, 1904), II, 47.

114. John Case as quoted in James E. Phillips, "Poetry and

Music in the Seventeenth Century," *Music and Literature in England in the Seventeenth and Eighteenth Centuries* (Los Angeles, 1953), p. 7.

115. Joseph Kerman, *The Elizabethan Madrigal* (New York, 1962), p. 70.

116. *Ibid.,* p. 6.

117. *Ibid.,* p. 48.

    E. H. Fellowes, *The English Madrigal Composers* (2d ed.; London, 1949), p. 37.

118. Tyard as quoted in Phillips, p. 4.

    Quoted in Phillips, p. 4.

119. Kerman, pp. 17–18.

120. Phillips, p. 7.

121. Kerman, pp. 33–34.

123. E. H. Fellowes, Preface to First Edition, *English Madrigal Verse: 1588–1632* (Oxford, 1929), pp. xiii–xiv.

124. Fellowes (1949), pp. 37–38.

125. *Ibid.,* p. 42.

126. Thomas Morley, *A Plain and Easy Introduction to Practical Music,* ed. R. Alec Harman (London, 1952), pp. 292–293.

127. Fellowes (1929), p. xvi.

    Kerman, p. 26.

128. Wilfrid Mellers, "Words and Music in Elizabethan England," in *The Age of Shakespeare,* ed. Boris Ford (Penguin Books, 1955), p. 401.

131. E. I. Watkin, *Catholic Art and Culture* (New York, 1944), p. 130.

    Knud Jeppesen, *The Style of Palestrina and the Dissonance,* tr. Margaret Hamerdik and Annie I. Fausbøll (2d ed.; London, 1946), p. 17n.

132. Blume, p. 90.

133. Roland Barthes, *Writing Degree Zero*, tr. Annette Levers and Colin Smith (New York, 1968), p. 4.

Gustave Reese, *Music in the Renaissance* (2d ed.; New York, 1959), p. 867.

134. Fellowes (1949), pp. 30–31.

135. Thomas Campion, *Campion's Works*, ed. Percival Vivian (Oxford, 1909), p. 4.

137. George T. Wright, *The Poet in the Poem* (Berkeley, 1960), p. 34.

139. *Ibid.*, p. 44.

140. *Ibid.*, p. 46.

141. Sidney in Smith, I, 183.

143. Jean Robertson, "Sir Philip Sidney and His Poetry," in *Elizabethan Poetry* (Stratford-upon-Avon Studies, No. 2; London, 1960), p. 119.

C. S. Lewis, *English Literature in the Sixteenth Century* (Oxford, 1954), pp. 327–328.

145. S. T. Coleridge, *Biographia Literaria*, ed. J. Shawcross (Oxford, 1907), II, 23–24.

146. James Joyce, "A Portrait of the Artist as a Young Man," in *The Portable James Joyce*, ed. Harry Levin (New York, 1947), p. 481.

147. T. S. Eliot, "Ulysses, Order, and Myth," *The Dial*, LXXV (1923), 483.

❧ *Chapter Five:* John Donne

*Page*

149. Ernst Cassirer, *Language and Myth*, tr. Susanne K. Langer (New York, 1946), p. 33.

150. Erwin Panofsky, *Idea*, tr. Joseph Peake (Columbia, S.C., 1968), p. 62.

151. Quoted in *Discussions of John Donne*, ed. Frank Kermode (Boston, 1962), p. 10.

Redpath as quoted in *John Donne's Poetry*, ed. A. L. Clements (New York, 1966), p. 205.

152. Aristotle, *The Rhetoric of Aristotle*, tr. Lane Cooper (New York, 1960), pp. 197–198.

153. H. M. Richmond, *The School of Love* (Princeton, 1964), p. 100.

De Quincey as quoted in Kermode, p. 17.

Grierson as quoted in Clements, p. 20.

154. Melton as quoted in Kermode, p. 128.

Arnold Stein, *John Donne's Lyrics* (Minneapolis, 1962), pp. 80–81.

155. Leavis as quoted in *Seventeenth-Century English Poetry*, ed. William R. Keast (Galaxy Books, 1962), p. 32.

Hallett Smith, *Elizabethan Poetry* (Cambridge, Mass., 1952), p. 289.

157. Stein, p. 169.

160. Sir Herbert Grierson, Introduction, *Donne: Poetical Works* (London, 1933), p. xxiii.

Andrews Wanning, Introduction, *Donne* (Dell Books, 1962), p. 14.

161. C. S. Lewis as quoted in Keast, p. 95.

Rosemund Tuve, *Elizabethan and Metaphysical Imagery* (Chicago, 1947), p. 264.

162. Johnson as quoted in Kermode, p. 7.

Symons as quoted in Kermode, p. 34.

163. Eliot as quoted in Keast, p. 27.

Tuve, p. 176.

164. Ignatius as quoted in Louis L. Martz, *The Poetry of Meditation* (New Haven, 1954), p. 27.

166. Walker as quoted in Keast, pp. 191, 187.

167. John Williams, Preface, *English Renaissance Poetry* (Anchor Books, 1963), p. xxv.

C. V. Wedgwood, *Seventeenth-Century English Literature* (Galaxy Books, 1961), p. 64.

169. Edmund Wilson, *Axel's Castle* (New York, 1931), pp. 107–108.

Eliot as quoted in Keast, pp. 26, 27.

170. Eliot as quoted in Clements, p. 133.

171. Robert Lowell, "Prose Genius in Verse," *Kenyon Review,* XV (1953), 620.

Robert Lowell, "A Note," *Kenyon Review,* VI (1944), 584.

T. S. Eliot, *On Poetry and Poets* (New York, 1957), p. 182.

Robert Lowell, Interview in the *Paris Review,* XXV (1961), 64–65.

172. *Ibid.,* 68.

Oscar Wilde, *The Artist as Critic,* ed. Richard Ellmann (New York, 1969), p. 320.

174. Allan Seager, *The Glass House* (New York, 1968), pp. 70, 85, 109.

176. Leslie A. Fiedler, "The Believing Poet and the Infidel Reader," *New Leader,* XXX (May 10, 1947), 12.

177. W. C. Williams, *Selected Letters,* ed. John C. Thirlwall (New York, 1957), p. 155.

Fiedler, p. 12.

178. W. D. Snodgrass, "Finding a Poem," *Partisan Review,* XXVI (1959), 283.

George T. Wright, *The Poet in the Poem* (Berkeley, 1960), p. 46.

Joseph Bennett, "Two Americans, a Brahmin and the Bourgeoisie," *Hudson Review,* XII (1959), 435.

179. Robert Lowell, Introduction, *Ariel,* by Sylvia Plath (New York, 1966), pp. ix–x.
George Herbert Mead, *Mind, Self and Society* (Phoenix Books, 1962), p. 158.
180. Ezra Pound, *Gaudier-Brzeska* (New York, 1916), p. 98.
Wright, p. 156.
181. John Berryman, Note, *His Toy, His Dream, His Rest* (New York, 1968), p. ix.
184. Wedgwood, p. 65.
W. C. Williams, p. 126.

# Bibliography

Alighieri, Dante. *A Translation of the Latin Works,* ed. A. G. Ferrers Howell. London, 1940.

Alpert, Harry. *Emile Durkheim and His Sociology.* New York, 1939.

Aristotle. *The Rhetoric,* tr. Lane Cooper. New York, 1960.

Atkins, J. W. H. *English Literary Criticism: The Medieval Phase.* Cambridge, 1934.

Auden, W. H. "John Skelton," in *The Great Tudors,* ed. Katherine Garvin. London, 1935.

St. Augustine. "On Music," tr. R. C. Taliaferro, in Volume IV of *The Fathers of the Church,* ed. Ludwig Schopp et al. New York, 1947.

Bainton, Roland. *The Reformation of the Sixteenth Century.* Boston, 1952.

Baldi, Sergio. *Sir Thomas Wyatt,* tr. F. T. Prince. London, 1961.

Barthes, Roland. *Writing Degree Zero,* tr. Annette Levers and Colin Smith. New York, 1968.

Bennett, Joseph. "Two Americans, a Brahmin and the Bourgeoisie," *Hudson Review,* XII (1959), 431–439.

Bergin, Thomas. Introduction to *Lyric Poetry of the Italian Renaissance,* ed. L. R. Lind. New Haven, 1954.

Berryman, John. *His Toy, His Dream, His Rest.* New York, 1968.

Bespaloff, Rachel. *On the Iliad,* tr. Mary McCarthy. Harper Torchbooks, 1962.

Bethell, S. L. "The Nature of Metaphysical Wit," *Northern Miscellany of Literary Criticism,* I (1953), 19–40.

Blume, Friedrich. *Renaissance and Baroque Music,* tr. M. D. Herter Norton. New York, 1967.

St. Bonaventure, *Meditations on the Life of Christ,* tr. Sister. M. Emmanuel, O.S.B. St. Louis, 1934.

Boyd, M. C. *Elizabethan Music and Musical Criticism.* 2d ed. Philadelphia, 1962.

Broadbent, J. B. *Poetic Love.* London, 1964.

Burckhardt, Jacob. *The Civilization of the Renaissance in Italy,* tr. S. G. C. Middlemore. New York, 1954.

Burr, Anna Robeson. *The Autobiography.* Boston, 1909.

Burton, Robert. *The Anatomy of Melancholy,* ed. Holbrook Jackson. London, 1932. 3 vols.

Bush, Douglas. *The Renaissance and English Humanism.* Toronto, 1939.

Campion, Thomas. *Campion's Works,* ed. Percival Vivian. Oxford, 1909.

Cassirer, Ernst. *The Individual and the Cosmos in Renaissance Philosophy,* tr. Mario Domandi. Harper Torchbooks, 1963.

——. *Language and Myth,* tr. Susanne K. Langer. New York, 1946.

Coleridge, S. T. *Biographia Literaria,* ed. J. Shawcross. Oxford, 1907. 2 vols.

Copland, Aaron. *Music and Imagination.* Mentor Books, 1959.

Cox, R. G. "A Survey of Literature from Donne to Marvell" in *From Donne to Marvell*, ed. Boris Ford. Penguin Books, 1956.

Cruttwell, Patrick. "Physiology and Psychology in Shakespeare's Age," *Journal of the History of Ideas*, XII (1951), 75–89.

Davis, Robert Gorham. "The New Criticism and the Democratic Tradition," *American Scholar*, XIX (1949–1950), 9–19.

De Quincey, Thomas. *Works*. Edinburgh, 1862.

Donaldson, E. Talbot. "The Myth of Courtly Love," *Ventures*, V (1965), 16–23.

"Donne's Poems," *Retrospective Review*, VIII (1823), 31–55.

Eliot, T. S. *On Poetry and Poets*. New York, 1957.

——. *Selected Essays*. London, 1951.

——. "Donne in Our Time," in *A Garland for John Donne*, ed. Theodore Spencer. Gloucester, Mass., 1931.

——. "Ulysses, Order, and Myth," *The Dial*, LXXV (1923), 480–483.

Evans, Maurice. *English Poetry in the Sixteenth Century*. 2d ed. New York, 1967.

Fellowes, E. H. *The English Madrigal Composers*. 2d ed. London, 1949.

——. *English Madrigal Verse: 1588–1632*. Oxford, 1929.

Fiedler, Leslie A. "The Believing Poet and the Infidel Reader," *New Leader*, XXX (May 10, 1947), 12.

Finney, Gretchen. *Musical Backgrounds for English Literature: 1580–1650*. New Brunswick, 1961.

Fowler, Alastair. *Spenser and the Numbers of Time*. New York, 1964.

Froude, James A. *Life and Letters of Erasmus*. New York, 1896.

Garside, Charles, Jr. *Zwingli and the Arts.* New Haven, 1966.

Gilbert, Neal Ward. *Renaissance Concepts of Method.* New York, 1960.

Gombrich, E. H. *Art and Illusion.* 2d ed. New York, 1961.

Grant, Robert M. *A Short History of the Interpretation of the Bible.* London, 1965.

Greene, Richard Leighton, ed. *Early English Carols.* Oxford, 1935.

Grierson, Sir Herbert. *Metaphysical Lyrics & Poems of the Seventeenth Century.* Oxford, 1921.

——. Introduction to *Donne: Poetical Works.* Oxford, 1933.

Hall, Vernon. *Renaissance Literary Criticism.* New York, 1945.

Haskins, Charles Homer. *The Renaissance of the Twelfth Century.* Cambridge, Mass., 1939.

Henderson, Philip, ed. *The Complete Poems of John Skelton.* London, 1948.

Hieatt, A. Kent. *Short Time's Endless Monument.* New York, 1960.

Hodgart, M. J. C. "Medieval Lyrics and the Ballads," in *The Age of Chaucer,* ed. Boris Ford. Penguin Books, 1954.

Hollander, John. *The Untuning of the Sky.* Princeton, 1961.

Howell, Wilbur Samuel. *Logic and Rhetoric in England, 1500–1700.* New York, 1961.

Ing, Catherine. *Elizabethan Lyrics.* London, 1951.

Jeppesen, Knud. *The Style of Palestrina and the Dissonance,* tr. Margaret W. Hamerdik and Annie I. Fausbøll. 2d ed. London, 1946.

John, Lisle. *The Elizabethan Sonnet Sequence.* New York, 1938.

Joyce, James. *The Portable James Joyce,* ed. Harry Levin. New York, 1947.

Kalstone, David. *Sidney's Poetry.* Cambridge, Mass., 1965.

Kerman, Joseph. *The English Madrigal.* New York, 1962.

Kocher, Paul H. *Science and Religion in Elizabethan England.* San Marino, Cal., 1953.

Kristeller, Paul Oskar. *Renaissance Thought.* Harper Torchbooks, 1961.

——. "Music and Learning in the Early Italian Renaissance," in *Renaissance Thought* II. Harper Torchbooks, 1965.

Leavis, F. R. *Revaluation: Tradition & Development in English Poetry.* London, 1936.

Lee, Sidney. *Elizabethan Sonnets.* Westminster, 1904. 2 vols.

LeHuray, Peter. *Music and the Reformation in England, 1549–1660.* New York, 1967.

Lever, J. W. *The Elizabethan Love Sonnet.* London, 1956.

Lewis, C. S. *The Allegory of Love.* Oxford, 1936.

——. *English Literature in the Sixteenth Century.* Oxford, 1954.

Lowell, Robert. Interview in the *Paris Review,* XXV (1961), 56–95.

——. Introduction to Sylvia Plath's *Ariel.* New York, 1966.

——. "A Note," *Kenyon Review,* VI (1944), 583–586.

——. "Prose Genius in Verse," *Kenyon Review,* XV (1953), 619–625.

Lowes, John Livingston. "The Loveres Maladye of Hereos," *Modern Philology* (1914), 491–546.

Lowinsky, E. E. *Secret Chromatic Art in the Netherlands Motet,* tr. Carl Buchman. New York, 1946.

Mackerness, E. D. *A Social History of English Music.* Toronto, 1964.

Martz, Louis L. *The Poetry of Meditation.* New Haven, 1954.

Mason, H. A. *Humanism and Poetry in the Early Tudor Court.* London, 1959.

Maynard, Winifred. "The Lyrics of Wyatt: Poems or Songs?" *Review of English Studies,* n.s. XVI (1965), 1–13.

Mazzeo, Joseph A. "Modern Theories of Metaphysical Poetry," *Modern Philology,* L (1952), 88–96.

Mead, George Herbert. *Mind, Self and Society.* Phoenix Books, 1962.

Mellers, Wilfrid. *Music and Society.* New York, 1950.

——. "Words and Music in Elizabethan England," in *The Age of Shakespeare,* ed. Boris Ford. Penguin Books, 1955.

Melton, Wightman Fletcher. *The Rhetoric of John Donne's Verse.* Baltimore, 1906.

Morley, Thomas. *A Plain and Easy Introduction to Practical Music,* ed. R. Alec Harmon. London, 1952.

Nelson, John Charles. *Renaissance Theory of Love.* New York, 1958.

Nelson, Norman. "Individualism as a Criterion of the Renaissance," *Journal of English and Germanic Philology,* XXXII (1933), 316–334.

Nietzsche, Friedrich. *The Birth of Tragedy,* tr. Francis Golffing. New York, 1956.

Osborn, James M., ed. *The Autobiography of Thomas Whythorne.* Oxford, 1962.

Panofsky, Erwin. *Idea,* tr. Joseph J. S. Peake. Columbia, S.C., 1968.

——. *Studies in Iconology.* Harper Torchbooks, 1962.

Phillips, James E. "Poetry and Music in the Seventeenth Century," in *Music & Literature in England in the Seventeenth and Eighteenth Centuries.* Los Angeles, 1953.

Pound, Ezra. *Gaudier-Brzeska.* New York, 1916.

Redpath, Theodore. Introduction to *The Songs and Sonnets of John Donne*. London, 1956.

Reese, Gustave. *Music in the Renaissance*. 2d ed. New York, 1959.

Richards, I. A. *Principles of Literary Criticism*. New York, 1924.

Richmond, Hugh M. *The School of Love*. Princeton, 1964.

Robbins, Rossell Hope. *Secular Lyrics of the XIVth and XVth Centuries*. Oxford, 1952.

Robertson, Jean. "Sir Philip Sidney and His Poetry," in *Elizabethan Poetry*. Stratford-upon-Avon Studies No. 2. London, 1960.

Rosenthal, M. L. "Poetry as Confession," *Nation*, CXC (1959), 154–155.

Sahlin, Margit. *Étude sur la carole médiévale*. Uppsala, 1940.

Scott, Izora. *Controversies over the Imitation of Cicero*. New York, 1910.

Seager, Allan. *The Glass House*. New York, 1968.

Seay, Albert. *Music in the Medieval World*. Englewood Cliffs, 1965.

Shumaker, Wayne. *English Autobiography*. Berkeley, 1954.

Singer, Irving. *The Nature of Love: Plato to Luther*. New York, 1966.

Smith, A. J. "The Metaphysic of Love," *Review of English Studies*, n.s. IX (1958), 362–375.

Smith, G. Gregory, ed. *Elizabethan Critical Essays*. London, 1904. 2 vols.

Smith, Hallett. *Elizabethan Poetry*. Cambridge, Mass., 1952.

Smith, James Harry, and Edd Winfield Parks, eds. *The Great Critics*. 3d ed. New York, 1951.

Snodgrass, W. D. "Finding a Poem," *Partisan Review*, XXVI (1959), 276–283.

Spiers, John. "A Survey of Medieval Verse," in *The Age of Chaucer,* ed. Boris Ford. Penguin Books, 1954.

Spingarn, Joel E. *Literary Criticism in the Renaissance.* Harbinger Books, 1963.

Stein, Arnold. *John Donne's Lyrics.* Minneapolis, 1962.

Stevens, John. *Music & Poetry in the Early Tudor Court.* London, 1961.

Symons, Arthur. "John Donne," *Fortnightly Review,* n.s. LXVI (1899), 734–745.

Swallow, Alan. "Skelton: The Structure of the Poem," *Philological Quarterly,* XXXII (1953), 29–42.

Tillyard, E. M. W. *The English Renaissance: Fact or Fiction?* London, 1952.

——, ed. *The Poetry of Sir Thomas Wyatt.* London, 1929.

Troeltsch, Ernst. *Protestantism and Progress,* tr. W. Montgomery. Beacon Paperbacks, 1958.

Trowell, Brian. "The Early Renaissance," in *The Pelican History of Music,* ed. Alec Robertson and Denis Stevens. Penguin Books, 1963. 2 vols.

Tuve, Rosemund. *Elizabethan and Metaphysical Imagery.* Chicago, 1947.

Valéry, Paul. "Introduction to the Method of Leonardo da Vinci," tr. Thomas McGreevy, *Selected Writings.* New York, 1950.

Van Doren, Mark. *Introduction to Poetry.* New York, 1968.

Walker, Ralph. "Ben Jonson's Lyric Poetry," *Criterion,* XIII (1933–1934), 430–448.

Wanning, Andrews, ed. *Donne.* Dell Books, 1962.

Watkin, E. I. *Catholic Art and Culture.* New York, 1944.

Wedgwood, C. V. *Seventeenth Century English Literature.* Galaxy Books, 1961.

White, Harold. *Plagiarism and Imitation during the English Renaissance*. Cambridge, Mass., 1935.

Wilde, Oscar. *The Artist as Critic*, ed. Richard Ellmann. New York, 1969.

Williams, John, ed. *English Renaissance Poetry*. Anchor Books, 1963.

Williams, William Carlos. *Selected Letters*, ed. John C. Thirlwall. New York, 1957.

Wilson, Edmund. *Axel's Castle*. New York, 1931.

Wright, George T. *The Poet in the Poem*. Berkeley, 1960.

# Index

*Transformations in the*
*Renaissance English Lyric*

Designed by R. E. Rosenbaum.
Composed by Vail-Ballou Press, Inc.,
in 11 point linotype Baskerville, 3 points leaded,
with display lines in monotype Baskerville 353.
Printed letterpress from type by Vail-Ballou Press
on Warren's No. 66 Text, 60 pound basis,
with the Cornell University Press watermark.
Bound by Vail-Ballou Press
in Interlaken ALA book cloth
and stamped in All Purpose black foil.